Siena
MY LOVE

Siena
MY LOVE

A NOVEL

TOM
BISOGNO

atmosphere press

Prologue

Michael Ventura was elated as he stood on stage after his last song. He took the time to introduce one of his favorite oldies, "The Way You Look Tonight." He told the attentive audience it was written in 1936 by Jerome Kern, with lyrics by Dorothy Fields. Michael added that it was first sung by Fred Astaire in the movie "*Swing Time*," which received an Academy Award. As he crooned it with great feeling, many of the women in the audience were moved emotionally. Michael glanced several times to his mom Manuela and his grandfather, Aurelio, who first inspired his interest in music. They were sitting next to their neighbor Sophia, a strikingly beautiful woman, and her son Michele. Sophia, a childhood friend, misted and wiped a tear as his romantic rendition brought back memories of their teenage friendship.

When he finished, Michael was overwhelmed by the standing applause of the sold-out Christmas fundraiser for several charities in Rome. The media had touted it as his come-back concert since Louisa. He bowed and blew kisses then went to the front of the stage to kneel and touch hands with some of his adoring fans. Several fans wanted him to accept gifts, and a few brought him food they made. One beautiful, exquisitely dressed woman tried to hand him a card that had her hotel and room number. Used to unexpected fan reactions, he thanked each one with a hand touch, as his security man followed closely and graciously accepted what was offered. He nodded his thanks and put each one carefully in a large white bag emblazoned with Italy's famous designer GUCCI.

Michael suddenly stood back up and raised his hands above his head and effusively thanked the audience for their support and generous donations. Slowly he backed up to the dark part of the stage, past the orchestra and the stage crew, and quickly retreated down the stairs to his dressing room.

Michael was totally exhausted from all the events since Louisa and returning to help his grandfather. As he sat on the couch and rested his head, Gerry Needham, his manager, came rushing in, beaming.

"Michael, you are back, big time...that was terrific...that last song was so moving, it had them on their feet at the end, and that duet with Vanessa had many of them in tears, including me. I was watching the guy from *Variety* over on stage left. He gave me a big thumbs up...boy you look really beat...you, okay?"

Michael had put his hand over his eyes.

"Gerry, I am so tired...I don't think I can sign five autographs without falling down. I also have a number of people, including Sophia, waiting to go to the hotel."

"You lie down, close your eyes and take a nap on that couch. I'll lock the door and handle everything...I'll get your family and Sophia and Michele back to the hotel and have the chauffeur wait by the loading dock, so you don't have to run a gauntlet when you leave."

"That's good...thanks."

4

Michael closed his eyes and tried to nap but began thinking about what brought him to this new turning point in his life and career. As his mind began to race, he suddenly remembered with a smile the time in Siena when he was fourteen and embarrassed by his reaction watching the Palio, as he looked out the window pressed against Sophia. His mind then shifted to his mother, Manuela, telling him at the hotel the story of how she first met his father, someone he missed terribly.

Chapter 1

IN THE BEGINNING WERE PARENTS

Michael Scott Rasmussen and Manuela Aurora Ventura met at St. John's University in Queens, NY, where she studied creative writing and he majored in marketing. Born in a small village near Siena, Italy, Manuela was raised on a vineyard and winery owned by her father, Aurelio. She came on a student visa to pursue her dream of being a writer. The two students met in an unusual way at a social gathering sponsored by his business club. Michael, a sophomore, first noticed freshman Manuela as she entered alone, and he couldn't take his eyes off of her. Many of the other young men stopped to stare at the beautiful eighteen-year-old with striking green eyes and long brown hair. Manuela was stunning in her form-fitting white dress that accented her bronzed skin and shapely figure. For Michael, she made all the other women at the event suddenly disappear.

When Manuela declined to dance with one of the aggressive young men, he became obnoxious. Michael, who was an imposing six foot two, moved quickly to intervene by inserting himself between the rude student and the lovely new arrival.

"Hey Jason...you're bothering my girlfriend...beat it, before I beat you."

"Sorry man...I didn't know."

As Jason quickly scurried away, Manuela chuckled at Michael's intervention.

"How did you know he would go quietly...or that I wouldn't say I'm not your girlfriend?"

"He's a bit of a jerk...thinks he's a lover but usually runs from any hint of rejection. He must have thought you were worth pressing. Frankly, I gambled you would be more interested in getting rid of him than outing me."

"You analyzed the situation well...you a psych major?"

"Marketing...we also have to analyze situations, make quick tactical decisions, and take risks...and I thought whatever happened, you were worth taking it."

"Well Mr. Gambling Man...I'm Manuela Ventura...since I've inherited a boyfriend I didn't know about; it might make sense to know his name."

"It's Michael Rasmussen. What heavenly place did Ms. Ventura come from, and what does she want to study at this great institution of learning?"

"I don't know if it qualifies as heavenly, but it is beautiful country. It's a small village near Siena, Italy. Ms. Ventura is hoping to develop her abilities in creative writing and improve her conversational English-speaking skills."

"It just so happens I am an expert in conversational English. Coincidentally, there is some less than satisfying non-alcoholic fruit punch over there where we can practice...although, frankly, you already speak like a native."

The two shared the punch that evening as well as several slow dances and ended up exchanging phone numbers that night. Within a month, the two were inseparable. Michael had fallen hard for the green-eyed beauty from Italy. He loved her assertive but upbeat gentle spirit and quick wit. She loved his quiet but take-charge nature and acerbic humor. It also didn't hurt that he was very good-looking. The two started dating casually but evolved quickly into a steady relationship, and by her sophomore year they were sharing an apartment off-campus. That became a little tricky whenever her dad, Aurelio, came to visit her and Michael had to quickly move in with a college buddy for the week.

On her graduation day, Manuela would soon be confronted with a decision to stay or leave, because her student visa would soon expire. Michael was already working as a market analyst in a major packaging firm. He had long decided to propose to Manuela at her graduation and combine the two memorable events. As Manuela, with tassel flying, was quickly leaving the stage at the graduation ceremony, Michael was blocking her exit at the bottom of the stairs. He smiled as she stopped, somewhat shocked that he was dramatically holding an engagement ring.

"Manuela Ventura, will you marry me?"

"You do know you are holding up a line of potentially violent students desperate to get through this ceremony."

"Say yes so everyone, especially me, will thank you."

"I guess you give me no choice. Put that damn ring on me and let everyone keep moving."

Michael put the ring on her finger and Manuela fell into his embrace and he carried her away to the applause and gratitude of all the graduates who were backed up on stage and the officials happy that the line was moving again.

Manuela quickly found a job as an entry-level trainee in a large advertising agency. Within two years, Michael was a marketing manager and Manuela was writing ad copy.

One evening when Michael arrived at their apartment after a late-night meeting, Manuela announced she was pregnant.

Chapter 2

MICHAEL'S EARLY DAYS

Manuela's pregnancy went well, and their family and friends were excited to meet the new boy that was imaged on the sonogram. When he was delivered, the baby arrived at a healthy seven pounds, eight ounces. His dad was there to also hold and hug his newborn. He was thrilled that Manuela was onboard to name the child Michael, which was a three-generation family name for male children. They readily agreed to name him Michael Joseph so that he would not be called Junior.

Manuela's father, Aurelio, flew in to see the boy baptized. He doted on the child for the week that he stayed and left a generous ten-thousand-dollar check and hoped they would visit him soon.

Because of work, financial reasons and other distractions, it took three years before they were to take Aurelio up on his invitation to visit. They were both excited to go on a much needed vacation to sunny Tuscany. Their flight on Alitalia to Rome was pleasant and made special when the flight attendant presented young Michael with a small plastic box containing a miniature commemorative captain's wing. She then brought him to see the cockpit, where the captain pinned the wings on the boy. Young Michael was so fascinated by the jetliner's instrument panel, the flight attendant had to get Manuela to pry him out of the cockpit.

Aurelio was thrilled to have his daughter's family stay with him at the farmhouse located on 14 hectares of vineyards with a small winery. After they were there for two days, Aurelio offered to take care of his grandchild so Manuela could show Michael Sr. all the amazing places in the region. It didn't take a minute for the parents to decide. Manuela always wanted to show off all the sites to her husband that she loved and introduce him to some relatives along the way.

While they toured Siena, Florence, and Lucca, and took a quick run up to Venice, Aurelio was spoiling young Michael by buying him toys, gelato and showing the child off to his neighbors. Maria and Francesco Mariano had a two-year-old girl named Sophia, who resented the visitor when her parents let the boy sit on her new pony. When the two-week vacation was over, Aurelio was very emotional as he hugged everyone goodbye. He hoped the family would come back soon and bring his wonderful grandson. Manuela promised she would, but she couldn't say when.

While Aurelio travelled to see them three times, Michael J. was 10 years old when Manuela was next able to take him to see his grandfather Aurelio. Since the last time that he visited the place was at three years old, the boy remembered little about that trip. He did still have the souvenir wings that the nice lady gave him, and memories of a nice pilot who let him see where they fly the plane. Not surprisingly, Michael J. didn't want to be away from his home for many reasons. He would miss his dad, his friends Don and Johnny, and his two-year-old pet Molly, a Soft-coated Wheaten Terrier. His father was now a Media Marketing Consultant who often worked out of the house. Michael Sr. always made time to play basketball in the driveway and go hiking with his son on special weekends in the Catskills.

Before young Michael left on his adventure with Mom to Italy, his dad took him on a very memorable hike in the dense forest deep in the Catskills. Their always-game pet Molly would run ahead then return, only to run ahead again. It was her way to play, which made the two Michaels smile and then chase her. Molly loved the chase but was much too fast to ever be caught, and quickly tired out her human playmates. Michael and his dad stopped to watch a herd of deer nearby, moving quickly away from the direction they were heading. They sensed that they may be running from danger and became concerned that Molly could be heading toward danger. They immediately increased their walking pace to find her. In the distance, their furry friend was barking loudly and repeatedly, as if in a frenzy. Since it was not something she normally did, they started running toward the sound.

As they reached a small clearing with several picnic tables, they spotted Molly in a standoff with a large black bear. The two were apparently in a dispute as to who should get to eat a thoughtless visitor's improperly discarded lunch.

"Holy shit, Dad...that bear will tear Molly apart."

"Watch your language, Michael, and don't do anything to excite the bear."

Young Michael, afraid for his scrappy terrier's safety, started to run toward the combatants. His Dad quickly reached out and pulled him back.

"Stay quiet and raise your arms outward to make yourself look larger."

His father quickly took a can of bear spray out of his knapsack and pointed it in the bear's direction. Michael Sr. then took a small cassette player out in a flash. He played the heavy metal music he had previously recorded and raised his arms outwardly, growling loudly and mimicking Molly's barking. Young Michael joined his dad in mimicking the dog barking. Molly turned, confused by the father and son's strange actions, and dropped a large chicken leg that was with a half-eaten corn-on-the-cob. Their precious pet ran back to them as fast as her legs could take her. The bear quickly picked up the morsels and took off into the woods.

Michael Sr. led his son and pet back to the parking area as fast as their feet could move. Once in the car, Michael asked about his dad's strange actions. Michael Sr. explained that bears don't like the loud sounds of a barking dog because originally dogs were descended from wolf packs. The bear spray was a last-minute defense if the bear charged.

Michael pointed to his dad's cassette player.

"Why that type of music?"

Michael Senior smiled at his son then said with a straight face, "Oh...I knew this particular bear preferred country music."

Young Michael looked at his father quizzically then realized his dad was joking.

"So next time we come we have to hope we don't meet one who likes that music."

Michael Sr. put his hand on his son's shoulder. "No...we have to hope we never meet any more bears."

On the way home, they celebrated their adventure by stopping to buy ice cream and a special treat for Molly. They also agreed to not worry Manuela about hiking with bears in the forest.

Michael was so impressed by his dad's quick thinking and Molly's bravery that he wrote a short story for an English class about their hiking adventure.

Michael was finally convinced by his dad to go on the trip to Italy that summer while shooting hoops. His dad suddenly stopped dribbling the ball and pointed to the beautiful blue sky with the clouds slowly drifting by.

"Do you know how lucky you are, going to Italy? When you come back, you can tell your friends that you saw those clouds up close when you were flying over them."

"You think they'll give me one of those wings, so I can have a pair?"

"If they still have them, I bet if you ask, they will."

Chapter 3

THERE'S A GIRL AT OUR GATE

The day they were leaving for their vacation in Italy, things were a little frenzied. Michael was emotional, hugging his pet goodbye. When Manuela said it was time to go, Michael put on Molly's leash and brought her to sit with him in the backseat of their Jeep station wagon. They had decided to drop Molly off at Uncle Charlie's house in Queens, which was on the way to JFK International Airport. They did it so the pet would not have to wait in the car in the summer heat. Michael's older cousin Miriam came out to take Molly and wished them a good trip.

When the three reached the security checkpoint, their farewells caused some poignant moments between Michael and his dad and mom. Michael Sr. took his son by his shoulders.

"Give your grandad a hug for me; try to make new friends and learn some Italian."

Michael hugged his dad's leg and said he would. Michael Sr. then gave his wife a long kiss goodbye.

"Stay safe and come back soon...I'll miss you every day you're away."

Young Michael smiled, enjoying his parents being so affectionate even though they had been married a long time. After the emotional goodbyes, the two travelers went through security and on to the boarding area for their flight to Rome.

Though their flight initially was delayed, the rest of the trip was a pleasant experience. When they entered the Fiumicino terminal in Rome, Michael experienced a little culture shock by the diversity of languages as they went through customs.

The almost three-hour drive from Rome to the grandfather's farmhouse was uneventful and mostly boring for the ten-year-old. He took out the wings he managed to get from a flight attendant, who brought them in a special promotional box along with a snack. It made him happy that he now had a pair of wings to show his friends.

Michael sat up and paid attention as they reached the pastoral Tuscany countryside. He enjoyed looking out the window at the changing hills and valleys. The landscape was filled with interesting fields, farms, vineyards and old buildings. Michael was still wide awake when they drove onto the Ventura Winery property. As they passed by the rows of vines and grapes, he became curious about what they did with all those grapes. He became excited when he spotted several rabbits running through the grapevines. Later he saw a squirrel and another, larger creature he found out later was a badger. It began to look like an interesting place to explore, but Michael began to wonder if there were anyone his age to play with.

The car drove on the gravel driveway for over a thousand feet. Finally, they arrived at the grandfather's farmhouse, which was over 300 years old. To Michael, the stone exterior looked different from the outside of any house he had ever seen. His grandfather, Aurelio, an energetic, well-built, tall man, was outside waiting and ushered them to come inside. When they entered, Michael was surprised that the house interior was normal looking. Aurelio hugged and kissed him on both cheeks and said he was so happy to see him.

"You have grown so much since I saw you the last time you were here."

Michael shrugged, not knowing what to say as he watched his mom kiss and hug her dad.

"He is getting to be a big, handsome, young man, isn't he?"

Manuela gave her dad an appraising look.

"It's in his genes to be good looking, like my father."

Aurelio waved at her to stop flattering him.

"Ah...he gets them from my beautiful daughter."

Manuela gripped her father's shoulder.

"Abbastanza...we'll just agree that we all did our part."

Their relaxed way of talking and touching reminded Michael of his own father's affectionate nature. Aurelio proudly gave them a quick tour of the improvements he made. He told them he had decided to renovate the old place two years ago. He wanted to update it so his lovely daughter and grandson would be happy to visit him. Proudly, he showed off his modern, well-equipped kitchen and the two renovated bathrooms with tubs and updated showers. Aurelio was particularly excited to show Michael his room, which was painted blue and refurbished with a new bed and a matching chest of drawers. The walls were decorated with lots of soccer and basketball sports memorabilia pictures. Michael nodded and smiled when his grandfather asked if he liked it.

"You kidding? This is nicer than my room at home. Thank you."

"So, tell me...how was the trip on the airplane?"

"We didn't see much...it was dark outside...there was a nice flight attendant who gave me some snacks and a set of wings...now I have a pair...then I fell asleep until we landed."

"What's your favorite foods?"

"I like lots of things...but I don't like weird-looking stuff."

Aurelio smiled and looked over at Manuela, who just shrugged and made a hand gesture that said "Don't look at me."

"What do you like to do when you're not in school?"

"Regular stuff. I play basketball with my friends, watch college football on TV. I really like reading books about space travel. I like to run and go biking to the park for exercise. Oh, and I like hiking with my dad and playing with my dog Molly... That's pretty much it."

Aurelio seemed to enjoy listening to his grandson. "Thank you, Michael. After lunch I'll show you what I like to do. But first, we eat."

They all sat down together for a lunch with an array of cold cuts, fresh fruit and bread that Aurelio had baked for the occasion. After they finished, Aurelio served espresso coffee to Manuela and brought a glass of cold milk, which he bought from a farmer friend especially for Michael. He went over to a kitchen cabinet and brought out a ciambellone ring cake. Michael hesitated at first but then took a small piece and after tasting it went back for more.

After lunch, as promised, Aurelio brought Michael into his office and introduced him to his old Victrola record player. It had a modern sound system connected to it, which fascinated Michael. Aurelio then introduced his grandson to an eclectic collection of old vinyl records: jazz music by Miles Davis, Duke Ellington and Ella Fitzgerald; opera singers like Caruso, Pavarotti and the young Andrea Bocelli; as well as popular American crooners like Bing Crosby, Frank Sinatra, Dean Martin and Tony Bennet. After Aurelio played a selection of different musical genres, he looked at his grandson.

"What do you think about the music? Did you like it?"

"Yeah...liked that jazz stuff...and I freakin' really liked some of those old songs. The music was nice. They're easy to listen to... Could I sometimes play your records? They're different than the stuff at home we listen to."

Aurelio smiled and put a hand on Michael's shoulder.

"My records are your records. but you shouldn't say that 'F' word. It can become a habit and be offensive."

Michael didn't think he had said something bad. "I think you thought I said the other bad 'F' word."

"Remember, if it even sounds like one, someone important to you someday might misunderstand and be offended. It's best to avoid any bad words. When I was a teenager, I cursed and swore because that's what kids did. One day my girl-friend's father heard me and he wouldn't let her go out with me after that. I had to wait until she was twenty-one before I could see her without her father knowing."

"What happened then?"

Aurelio smiled and put his hand on Michael's shoulder. "I married her."

Michael laughed and gave Aurelio a big hug. Michael was curious about what happened to his grandmother but didn't want to upset his grandfather by asking him. He looked forward to finding out more about his family. That night, Michael slept well, until he was awakened early in the morning by the birds and noise from the grape pickers working in the nearby vineyard.

After their talk at breakfast, Aurelio sensed that Michael felt out of place because the vineyard was so far from everything that it may not be fun for a ten-year-old boy. He called his maintenance man and told him to find and install a basketball set and put it in by the garage area. Aurelio took Michael under his wing to show him how the vineyard provided the grapes to make the wine. He then introduced him to his winemaker, Pietro, who did speak English. Michael became fascinated with the wine-making process and asked to hang out with Pietro, who taught him how the grapes were processed and the various steps to turn them into wine. He even let Michael sample the wine on a spoon. Michael screwed up his nose.

"It tastes funny to me."

Pietro laughed and shook hands with Michael. "When I was your age, it tasted funny to me."

Excited about what he learned, Michael came back to the farmhouse to ask his grandfather more questions about how the wine got from this place to the stores near his house. Aurelio explained the way distribution worked in very simple terms so the curious ten-year-old would understand the basics. The grandfather described on a piece of paper the wine's movement from his place to the store in Michael's neighborhood.

Michael thought it was pretty cool the way everything came to together and ended up in a liquor store near his house. Aurelio, happy that his grandson took an interest in his business, suggested they take a break and have a treat. All Michael wanted was a piece of the bread Aurelio had baked, so the two feasted together on the bread, slathered generously with grape preserves from the Ventura vineyard.

Since Manuela had gone to the local village to visit an old friend from her childhood, Aurelio wanted to keep Michael occupied so he suggested they listen to more of his music collection. Despite their significant age difference, the two found a special bond listening to the old standards. When no one was around, Michael would go there and play the old romantic songs, and even learned some of the lyrics. Somehow the old music and songs appealed to him and he started to sing along with his favorite tunes.

By the fourth day of the visit, Michael began to feel comfortable enough to explore the property on his own. He ran along the paths between the grapevines and jumped up and down at the end of each row as if he won a race. He was enjoying the fresh air and freedom to roam on his own. He made it a game to see how fast he could run the rows. Using the second hand on the watch that his dad bought him for his birthday as a timer, he tried to beat the running time of the prior row. When he ran to the end of the last row, he stopped short. There was a young girl swinging on a connecting gate. Upset that some stranger was coming onto his grandfather's land, he yelled at her.

"What are you doing here?"

Sophia Mariano was a precocious nine-year-old who lived with her family on the neighboring vineyard, and the gate enabled both sides easy walking access to the other. She did not take kindly to the strange boy who was trespassing on her neighbor's property and yelled back at him.

"Che hai detto?" (What did you say?)

Not understanding her and still thinking she was either trespassing or was there to steal, Michael went to the gate and confronted her up close.

"You better leave now, or I'll call the police."

(È meglio che te ne vai adesso o chiamo la polizia.)

Sophia looked at Michael confused by what he said in English.

"Ah, sì...ora vado a chiamare la polizia." (Ah yes...I go now to call the police.)

Sophia wagged her finger at Michael and closed the gate, making a point of clicking it shut, then ran off. Michael shrugged and headed back, believing he had scared the intruder who really believed that he was calling the police.

Aurelio had wondered where Michael was and thought about looking for him when the phone rang. He picked it up. It was his neighbor, Maria.

"Ti chiamo perché Sophia ha visto un ragazzo strano nella

tua proprietà che le ha detto di chiamare la polizia." (Hi Aurelio...I'm calling because Sophia saw a strange boy on your property who told her to call the police.)

Aurelio shook his head, confused, but then, realizing what probably happened, chuckled into the phone. "Maria...that boy was my grandson, Michael. He's visiting with his mother Manuela."

Maria smiled, realizing Sophia probably misunderstood the boy.

"Devi venire a cena domani sera così li facciamo incontrare." (You must come to dinner tomorrow evening so we can meet them.)

Aurelio thought for a moment about what happened.

"Verremo alle sette, così possiamo far conoscere a Michael la tua Sophia, così non chiama la polizia." (We will come at seven so we can have Michael meet your Sophia, so she doesn't call the police.)

The two neighbors both laughed heartily and hung up.

When the two children were formally introduced, the real truth about their misunderstanding was clarified. Sophia giggled about the incident and Michael just shook his head, still thinking the girl was a little nuts. Maria told the children they had met before, but Sophia didn't like Michael to sit on her pony. Neither of them remembered the incident.

Still wary of each other, Sophia asked how old Michael was now by pointing to herself and showing nine fingers. Michael understood and held up ten fingers. Both could see that while the language barrier posed an obstacle in getting to know each other, there were ways to communicate without words.

The adults wanted to talk so they encouraged the children to go outside. Maria suggested Sophia show Michael her horse. They looked at each other and shrugged then Sophia signaled for Michael to follow her. Once outside, she indicated with her finger to go toward some outbuildings. Michael followed

Sophia into a stable where she kept her horse named Bellino (pretty). Michael was fascinated as Sophia talked gently to her and fed her a carrot that she managed to sneak out of the kitchen. He looked at his grandfather's young neighbor with new eyes when she taught Michael how to groom Bellino. Using a brush, he gently followed her lead, and the filly responded by nudging him with her nose, which made him smile. Sophia led Bellino outside and tied her reins to a fence, then showed Michael how to clean out the horse's stall. As Michael and Sophia worked and played together, they slowly developed an unusual friendship.

They began to understand each other by using facial expressions, hand gestures and body language. During Michael's visit, Sophia taught him some Italian words and he taught her English words. She showed him how to kick a soccer ball while he showed her how to play basketball on the court that Aurelio just had built for him. When Sophia encouraged Michael to ride Bellino, he hesitated. Sophia realized that Michael he didn't know how to ride a horse and indicated they could ride together. He nodded to say he would give it a try and after a few false starts, he mounted the horse by first climbing on a bag of hay.

With Sophia controlling the reins, the two rode together through the undeveloped fields and by a small lake on the adjoining property. Sophia told him in their made-up sign language that it was owned by a rich German who only came to live in the big villa occasionally. He didn't understand all the things she said so after he was back, he asked his mom to tell him what she knew. Manuela told him pretty much what Sophia tried to tell him, except that she added that his grandfather was a friend of the owner. Michael was surprised by how much he and Sophia understood each other.

One of the favorite past times for Sophia and Michael was to go into Aurelio's office and listen to his record collection.

They would sometimes listen for hours to the old songs in Italian and English. While Sophia didn't understand many of the English lyrics, she loved the melodies. After they played some of Michael's favorites a few times, he began to sing along, which made her smile. On one of the songs about love, he mimicked the singer's sensual delivery of the lyrics and Sophia giggled.

On hot days, they would go swimming in their underwear in the small lake they found. The third time they approached the lake on foot, they had to retreat quickly. From behind a large tree, they saw the property's caretaker standing where they usually entered the water. He was holding a candy wrapper they apparently had not taken away. He began talking to himself in a loud voice.

"C'era qualcuno che nuotava nel nostro lago. Che faccio chiamo la polizia?" (Someone's been swimming in our lake. Should I call the police?)

Sophia's eyes widened. She put her finger up to her lips for him to be quiet then grabbed Michael's hand. The caretaker smiled as he turned to watch the two intruders run as fast as their legs could carry them back to the safety of Sophia's vineyard. They didn't go back to swim the rest of Michael's visit.

The three-week visit went by so quickly, Michael was surprised when Manuela told him they needed to start packing. She said they had to leave the next day to catch their flight out of Rome. While Michael was happy to go home and see his dad and pet, he told his Mom he was sad to leave his new friend, even though she was a girl. Manuela showed him her translation book she used in high school. She suggested Michael try using it when he was with Sophia. When he used it to translate for Sophia the news that they were leaving, she was heartbroken and sorry he couldn't stay longer. She asked in Italian and gestures if he would ever be back. He understood her gestures, which had become their special sign language.

"I'll try to come back. When I do, I will bring you a special present."

Sophia put up her hands, indicating she didn't understand. "Non capisco."

Michael took out his mother's book. When he showed her the translation, her eyes lit up. After writing down a translation, she pointed to Michael and then to herself.

"Sarò la tua ragazza...mi porti un regalo?" (I will be your girlfriend...you bring me a present?)

After roughly translating what she said by painfully looking up the words, he shrugged and resorted to using their personal sign language. "I guess so...you are my friend, and you are a girl."

Sophia smiled broadly after reading some of the words and gave him a kiss on the cheek then ran back along the rows of grapes and through their meeting gate. Michael stood there wondering if the translation was what he said and didn't translate into something crazy.

Sophia ran as fast as she could into the Mariano vineyard and was jumping up and down excitedly. Her father wondered why his nine-year-old daughter was so happy. Francesco left his men and grabbed Sophia by her shoulders to stop her from jumping up and down.

"Figlia mia che è successo?" (My child, what has happened?)

"Papà, Michael mi porterà un regalo e sarò la sua ragazza." (Father, Michael will bring me a present and I will be his girlfriend.)

"Bimba mia, te tu c'hai solo nove anni...devi aspettare di essere molto più grande per essere la sua ragazza." (My girl, you are only nine years old...you must wait until you are much older to be a girlfriend.)

"Sì papà, lo so...solo quando mi porterà un regalo." (Yes,

father I know....only when he brings me a present.)

Several of his men who were listening started to laugh because of his frustration trying to talk to his young daughter.

Francesco threw up his hands. "Madre di Dio, cosa devo fare con questa bambina?" (Mother of God, what do I do with this child?)

Sophia looked at her father like he didn't understand. "Dovrei parlare con la mamma del regalo?" (Should I talk to mother about the present?)

Francesco sighed. "Sì, per favore parla con tua madre." (Yes, please talk to your mother.)

As Sophia skipped away happily, Francesco tapped the front of his head with his knuckles.

"Figlie!" (Daughters!)

The next day, Sophia came to say goodbye with her mom. After Aurelio helped Manuela load the car with the luggage, he embraced her, then made her promise to come back to see him next summer. He kissed Michael on both cheeks and said he looked forward to seeing him next year and hoped he would sing for him instead of waiting for everyone to leave before he did on his own.

"You heard?"

Aurelio nodded.

"I think you have a nice voice...you should develop it! Promise me you'll come back and sing for me."

Michael shrugged.

"You want me to?"

"I want you to."

Sophia watched the Ventura family say their loving farewells. When it looked like they were about to leave, she rushed up to Michael and hugged him tightly and gave him a piece of paper with her address, pointing to it and making a handwriting gesture.

"Mi scrivi?" (You write to me?)

Michael gave her an awkward hug back. "Okay."

"E mi porti un regalo?" (Bring present?)

Michael looked to his mother who mouthed "Present" to him. He shrugged and nodded. "Yes."

Manuela watched with Aurelio as the two children said their goodbyes and gripped her dad's arm.

"Michael's growing up. First time I saw him fond of a girl, much less even talk to one."

Aurelio grinned. "In a few years, he will be very interested in them, and the girls will be calling him and making you crazy."

Manuela grimaced at the thought of her little angel becoming a female magnet. Now she was happy he had a little friend next door so he wouldn't be resistant to visit his grandfather. As they drove away, Michael exchanged goodbye waves with Sophia but couldn't see her tears that were welling up.

Chapter 4

GROWING UP

Michael hugged his dad who picked them up at the airport. On the drive home, Michael Sr. brought them up to date on family and local news while they were away. As soon as they arrived, Michael took Molly on a long walk around the neighborhood. In the next few weeks, he resumed his life at home, connecting with his friends, especially Johnny and Don. Michael told them about his adventures flying over the clouds to Italy, learning about winemaking and riding a horse. He proudly showed them the pair of wings he was given on the plane rides. He omitted that he played with the neighbor girl because he didn't need to get ranked on by them. He was already looking forward to the hiking trips before the start of the fall term. Whenever they were deep on a wooded trail, he felt a little uncomfortable taking Molly off her leash because of their experience with the bear.

Michael was happy he had an adventure in Italy but glad to be home. Back in his room, he watched TV and played games on his father's old computer. Now he also liked listening to some of the old hit songs performed by their original singers. He enjoyed hearing their voices, the clear way they sang the lyrics and how different words were phrased for emphasis. When his dad listened with him, he told Michael that the songs were big hits in their day. He added that it would take someone with the voice and talent of those singers to make them hits again. From a marketing standpoint, that may be an opportunity for someone with the right talent. Michael shrugged but he thought it was interesting that such popular songs weren't still worth singing.

As Michael came down in the morning, his parents were talking seriously in the living room. He waited at the door until they finished their conversation. When Manuela saw him, she looked at him questioningly.

"What is it, Michael?"

"I just wanted to tell you when school starts this fall, I'm going to try harder to get better grades, even in subjects I really don't like. I think I would also like to learn more about music."

After his announcement, Michael quickly left the room. Michael Sr. turned to Manuela teasingly.

"Who was that kid? What did you do with our son?"

"Isn't he wonderful? He's growing up."

The next morning, Michael came down to breakfast. Manuela turned from what she was doing at the stove.

"Good morning, Michael."

"Could we also get someone to teach me Italian?"

"Don't they teach it at school?"

"No, Spanish and French are the only choices."

"I'll talk to your father. Maybe we can find a tutor."

Manuela was so pleased he wanted to learn her father's native language; she convinced his dad to hire a tutor. Because he and Sophia had promised to write each other, he sent her letters with a mix of Italian and English words. Sophia's letters at first were totally in Italian and he had to have Manuela translate. Over the next several months, her letters began to come written in in both Italian and English words. With the help of the tutor, Michael was able to understand many of the letters without asking his mom to translate. Sometimes Sophia wrote some gushy stuff. Michael didn't think Sophia knew what some of the words even meant. He had the tutor help him sprinkle in Italian expressions. To impress Sophia on his next visit, Michael went to high school soccer games and learned how many drop-back steps to take and some goal-kicking techniques.

That year at home passed quickly for Michael. He grew three inches and improved his school performance and ended up with all good grades on his report card. Manuela tried to convince her husband that the experience in Italy was part of his maturing. His dad was skeptical about that claim but believed intercultural experiences were an important part of learning.

Spring came and went. Before Michael knew it, school was over and summer vacation was on. Manuela had been pro-moting another three weeks in Italy. Finally, she had Michael Sr. on board. Manuela came to Michael's room where he was reading and coyly suggested if he was up to it, they could visit her father again. Michael looked up and smiled.

"When do we leave?"

As they planned their trip to Italy, Michael remembered his promise to bring Sophia a present. While shopping at the mall with his mom, he saw a charm bracelet with a silver horse that had a price tag of twenty-five dollars. He asked Manuela if she thought Sophia would like it. Manuela was surprised by her young son's thoughtfulness and offered to get it for him. He said he would pay for it and pulled out the cash he saved from his allowance and birthday. Manuela watched with admiration as he proudly paid for Sophia's present, had it gift wrapped, took the receipt and put it in the bag with the present.

During the weeks before the trip, the two Michaels went on a hike and to an amusement park. As a going-away sendoff, father and son shared a pizza and a movie. His dad felt sorry that he couldn't come with them, but his new client needed a market strategy and implementation within the month.

The day they went to the airport, Michael sensed some tension between his parents. Whatever was going on they kept to themselves. When the two were seated on the plane, Michael turned to his mom in deep thought.

"Mom, is everything all right?"

"Why do you ask?"

"You and Dad were acting weird on the way to the airport."

"It's nothing to worry about. Your father has some work pressures. He's dealing with them."

Michael looked worried. Manuela took his hand and squeezed it.

"I promise nothing is wrong. Let's have a nice visit with my dad, who is so excited to see you."

Michael nodded and smiled but was still concerned as the plane took off. The flight was on time and the drive to the grandfather's farmhouse uneventful. In fact, Michael slept a good part of the way.

When they arrived, Aurelio was outside, anxious to greet them. Next to him was an excited Sophia, who had grown taller and now had a ponytail instead of braids. After the initial hugs were over, Michael handed her his present. When she opened it, she was so happy she jumped up and down then gave Michael the biggest hug ever and kissed him on both cheeks. Manuela and Aurelio looked at each other then he leaned over and whispered.

"My grandson knows the way to a girl's heart and he's only

eleven... He didn't inherit that gene from me...I'm still clueless."

Manuela frowned at the thought. "Hmm...I'm going to have to ask his father what he knew about girls' hearts when he was eleven."

Manuela's wry sense of humor made Aurelio smile. "By any chance, were you very friendly with any of those door-to-door salesmen?"

Manuela punched Aurelio's arm playfully. "Dad! Don't even joke about that. One of my friends just got divorced because when her husband came home early, he found her with one of the men who delivered their couch."

Aurelio had a twinkle in his eye. "Sorry, I shouldn't joke about that kind of thing. I guess the man felt an obligation to deliver and test the goods."

Manuela pushed his arm again and made a "*Grrr*!" sound. "You are incorrigible."

Aurelio said he had prepared a lunch for everyone and escorted them into the house. They all trouped into his kitchen. Before he could ask the children what they wanted, the two young friends disappeared into the vineyard. They both walked along the paths between the grape bushes, bringing each other up to date on their last year. Sophia said she had been learning English from the high school language teacher who tutored on the side. She demonstrated how many words she learned, and he applauded her. Michael then reciprocated, impressing her with his fledgling Italian. They walked and talked for two hours. Even when they didn't quite understand what the other said, out of courtesy they acted like they did.

As they crossed into Sophia's side of the gate, she spotted her father with some of his workers. She ran up to him and showed him the beautiful bracelet that Michael gave her. Francesco looked at the gift and then at his little girl with some concern.

"Michael...la mia Sophie è ancora troppo giovane per regali così costosi." (Michael...my Sophie's still too young for such expensive presents.)

Sophie translated the words but both children didn't understand his concern. Michael thought her father thought it cost too much.

"It didn't cost that much... Only twenty-five dollars."

Francesco looked at Sophia questioningly. She thought for a minute trying to calculate in her mind.

"E'costato solo 20.000 lire." (It only cost 20,000 Lira.)

Francesco realized the children were too innocent to understand his concern, so he made out he was looking again at the gift.

"Cavallo molto carino."

Sophia translated into English for Michael. "Papa likes the cavalla."

Michael smiled and nodded to Francesco. "It reminded me of Bellino."

Exasperated that his concerns were not understood, Francesco turned to his men. "Torniamo a lavorare." (Let's get back to work.)

As they resumed their friendship that visit, Michael and Sophia became inseparable for the time he was there. Both families recognized their special relationship and took both with them on side trips to Siena, Orvieto and Montepulciano, but Michael couldn't go with them to Florence. Sophia was sad he couldn't come, and promised that when he came back someday, she would show him that beautiful city.

They resumed teaching each other about their native sports. Sophia was surprised how Michael had improved his soccer skills as he demonstrated what he learned at home, including his inside hook that she taught him. Sophia impressed him with her basketball shooting skills. Michael didn't know that she had been practicing on her own at Aurelio's.

When Sophia told her mother how they rode on the horse together, her mom asked Francesco to get another one for the children. Because he was old fashioned and didn't approve of Michael and Sophia sitting that close, he gladly bought a second horse so they would ride separately.

The next year that Michael visited Sophia, she was twelve. He was still somewhat clueless about how self-conscious young girls were about their changing physicality. When Michael suggested they ride over to the lake on a very hot day for a swim, she said she couldn't because her mother needed her help. Sophia went to Maria and told her that she didn't want to swim in her underwear and her old bathing suit didn't fit anymore. Maria understood and took her into Siena and bought her a proper one-piece bathing suit. The next hot day that Michael suggested they go for a swim, Sophia said she would go home and put on her new bathing suit. Michael, feeling self-conscious, also retreated to change into his modest swimming trunk, which Manuela bought for him before they left home. When they arrived at the lake to swim, they looked at each other and realized in some ways their bathing suits revealed more about their bodies than wearing their underwear. Sophia could see now see Michael's developing upper muscular physique because he was not wearing a tee shirt. Michael noticed the slightly more curvaceous nature of Sophia's emerging feminine body.

Realizing they were staring at each other, the two friends jumped into the cool lake water. Sophia felt the urge to get Michael's attention and splashed him when he wasn't looking. He retaliated and they quickly regressed into being kids again, splashing and making lots of noise. Sophia tried to escape Michael's unrelenting splashing attack by swimming back to shore while he swam across to the other side. As she arrived, she saw two shoes where she usually climbed out. The shoes were filled by a well-dressed, large man who bent down with his hand extended. He spoke English but with an accent Sophia didn't recognize.

"Young lady...do you need any help getting out?"

"Fo da sola." (I can do it myself.)

"Ah...Italiano...Ventura? Mariano?"

"Mariano...Sono Sofia!"

The man then pointed questioningly to Michael, who was swimming away from them.

"Michael è il nipote di Ventura."

Michael, who had started to swim across the lake for exercise, looked back to see where Sophia had gone. He saw the large man reaching for Sophia and began swimming as fast as he could back to shore. By the time he arrived at the exit point, Sophia and the man were sitting and talking. As Michael climbed out of the water, the man extended a handshake.

"Michael. Come and sit with Sophia. My name is Gerhard Schmidt. I own this property and understand you are the grandson of my friend Aurelio."

"Yes. Please don't tell him. We didn't break anything; we were only swimming and splashing."

Mr. Schmidt guffawed.

"Do not worry, young Michael. I was napping out by my garden, and I heard you having fun. My grandchildren used to come and swim. Now they are grown and away in college. I am not what you call a tattle-tale person."

"Sorry for making so much noise. We didn't think anyone was around."

"I came to get away from my work and rest. My villa is just on the other side of those trees. I needed the walking exercise, as you can tell, and I'm happy that somebody was enjoying the lake. I miss having my family visit here."

Michael became excited.

"We'd love to see your house. Your property is amazing and sort of a mysterious place."

Mr. Schmidt laughed.

"No mystery. It's old but I haven't seen any ghosts. Come, and I'll show you my beautiful gardens. When I used to stay longer, Aurelio would bring a bottle of his wine and I would bring different cheeses from my factories and we'd eat, drink and talk on the veranda. Sometimes we would get in a game of chess. I miss that."

Mr. Schmidt led the children through a wooded lined walking lane that ended at a large stone villa. Gerhard proudly showed them his garden, filled with beautiful red Tuscan poppies and a variety of roses. He picked two bunches and gave one to Sophia for her mom and one to Michael for his.

As the children returned to their respective homes, Michael was thoughtful and began smiling to himself thinking about it, then blurted out.

"Someday I'm going to buy a place like Mr. Schmidt, and I'll go there so I can rest like him."

Sophia began smiling too. "Can I visit you in your big house?"

"Of course, you're my friend. You will always be welcome."

Sophia smiled and took Michael's hand and led him as she skipped the rest of the way. They separated at the gate, and each went to their homes with the flowers.

When Michael entered the farmhouse, Manuela came over to see the beautiful flowers.

"Where did you find those beautiful poppies?"

"Mr. Schmidt, who lives on the big property next door, sent these for you."

"These are so gorgeous. His gardener is first class. I'll call him later to thank him."

Manuela found and started to put them in a vase.

Aurelio came over and touched the petals on the brilliant red poppies then smelled the roses. "These are perfect, Manuela. Gerhard and I used to have good times sharing wine and cheese. Why don't we pay him a visit instead of calling? You should see what he's done with his place."

Michael chimed in excitedly. "Can I come and bring Sophia? We didn't get to see inside his house. Someday I want to buy a place like his to have a place to rest."

Manuela and Aurelio did a double take but were impressed by young Michael's ambitious goal of owning a very expensive getaway property and nodded their approval.

"I will call Gerhard. You go get Sophia. I will bring wine and soft drinks and we'll all go see his wonderful old villa."

After returning from their collective visit to their neighbor's beautiful home, Michael agreed to sing one of his grandfather's favorite songs, "What a Wonderful World." Aurelio told him it was made famous by Louis Armstrong, a famous jazz singer and trumpeter. Aurelio, with tears in his eyes, confessed it was Michael's grandmother's favorite and became his favorite to remember her. When Michael started singing in an upbeat tempo, Aurelio joined him, surprising both his daughter and Sophia with his talent

After they performed the iconic hit song without missing a beat, Manuela and Sophia applauded the talented duo. Manuela whistled her approval and bear-hugged her dad and her son.

"Now I know where Michael's talent comes from."

Over the next weeks of Michael's visit, the children played the records for hours. Michael listened intently and learned the lyrics to many of the old hit songs by heart. What Michael wasn't aware of was that his twelve-year-old playmate had developed a big crush and watched him closely when he wasn't looking. Sophia's heart beat faster when he smiled at her or sang one of the romantic songs. By the end of that summer, she was so enamored with Michael that the girl sometimes couldn't sleep for thinking about him. He felt closer to Sophia than to his best friend back home but was still clueless about any childhood romantic feelings.

The night before Manuela and Michael had to return home that year, Sophia cried herself to sleep. Her mother noticed in the morning how red her eyes were and asked if she was sick. When she told Maria why, Sophia was discouraged from saying goodbye to Michael so she wouldn't be sad when he left. Sophia said she would be sadder if she didn't see him and ran next door. As her mother warned her, she lost it when the car taking Michael to Rome went out of site. Aurelio saw her reaction and went over to comfort her.

"Michael tornerà. So che prova qualcosa per te, su non piangere. Perché non vai a casa e gli scrivi una lettera cosi rimanete in contatto." (Michael will come back. I know he has feelings for you, so don't cry. Why don't you go home and write him a letter, so you both keep in touch?)

Sophia hugged Aurelio and her tears turned to sniffles as she ran home to write a letter.

Chapter 5

ADOLESCENCE AWAKENING SHATTERED

The very next year's summer visit completely changed their relationship from a childhood friendship to a sensual awareness of each other. Now fourteen, Michael was aware of his own physical sexual reactions. While Sophia was still his good friend, he began looking at her in a different way. On her part, Sophia felt she had to resist her schoolgirl romantic feelings for Michael, so it didn't affect their friendship. Both did not completely understand how the physical and psychological changes of adolescence were impacting them. They both felt something fundamental had happened, but they didn't quite understand it. When they jumped in the lake to swim, Michael felt a twinge looking at Sophia's budding breasts peeking out from under her bathing suit. Sophia was not only aware that Michael had grown tall, but his chest and stomach muscles were more prominent. She was not aware that Michael had masculine urges while she was also experiencing hormonal and physical desires of her own.

These feelings toward each other came to a head when

Michael accompanied his mother with Sophia's family to the Palio in Siena. They were invited to watch the iconic horse race around the square from her Uncle Rosario's apartment. Michael was fascinated by the pre-race activities, especially watching the colorful riders bring the horses into the church. He could feel the energy of the historic medieval city as it prepared for the anticipated national event. As he looked around at the buildings surrounding the square, he became excited that they would be able to watch the race from one of them.

Maria said they should move along, as they needed to get off the square shortly and to her brother's apartment. Uncle Rosario was a large man who welcomed them. He hugged and kissed everyone who came and invited them to eat and drink. Maria told Manuela that her brother Rosario owned a restaurant and had everything sent over. Michael and Sophia picked at the food on the table and when they thought no one was looking took some wine in a coffee cup to see how it tasted. It still tasted funny to them, both agreeing that adults have strange tastes. They ditched what was left in a flowerpot and went to find a soft drink.

When the race was about to start everyone ran to the windows to watch. Michael and Sophia decided to watch it from a smaller window together. To see the action, Michael had to squeeze against Sophia and put his arms on her shoulder then lean forward until their cheeks touched. He steadied himself by gripping her arms to look out the window at the horses racing around the square. Sophia felt that holding her was a sign of Michal's affection and leaned back against him, triggering an embarrassing physical reaction. The unexpected contact caused a wide-eyed Sophia to move forward and closer to the window.

Michael was so embarrassed. He said he was sorry and excused himself to go to the bathroom. He let out a big sigh, adjusted his clothes and put cold water on his face. While gathering his thoughts, Michael remembered his dad's talk to him about sex and being respectful to girls. He decided it would be better to watch the race from a large window alongside his mother. As he stood next to her, Manuela decided to confront the situation, which she had observed when she heard Michael say sorry and leave.

"Michael, I think that small window put you both in an awkward situation."

"Tell me about it."

"You didn't do anything wrong."

"Except make Sophie uncomfortable, and she probably won't like me anymore."

Manuela smiled. "I don't think that will ever happen. You'll see."

Sophia, not understanding Michael's dilemma, thought she had insulted him by moving away. She decided to avoid Michael until she could figure out what to do. On the way back to their respective vineyards, the car was unusually quiet except for the sound of breathing and the car's engine, as the two young friends thought about what to say to the other.

Once back to the farmhouse, Michael went right to his bedroom. While he avoided going to visit Sophia, thinking she would be mad at him, Sophia decided to have a serious conversation with her more worldly-wise older cousin Vittoria. When she described what happened, the sixteen-year-old was more than helpful.

"Non è niente, significa solo che gli piaci." (That's nothing. It only means he likes you.)

Unfortunately, before he could figure out what to say to his friend, Michael's summer visit was tragically cut short. As his mother answered the fateful call, Michael saw the look of shock on her face. His dad was in critical condition from a serious automobile accident. His car had been hit head-on by a drunk driver and he was in a critical care unit at the Westchester Medical Center. The tragic news caused Manuela and Michael to leave immediately for the airport in Rome without saying goodbye to Sophia.

Chapter 6

HARD TIMES

When Michael and his mom returned to JFK, they rushed directly to the hospital to see Michael Sr. They found him still in a coma, on life support, and were devastated when the surgeon told them he might not survive. Manuela sat and told him about their trip and how much they needed him to get well because they loved him so much. Michael said he and Molly looked forward to going out on hikes with him when he felt better. Tragically, young Michael never got to say how much he and his mom loved him. The two had to sit helplessly by his dad's bedside listening to the monitors trigger a code-four announcement over the ICU loudspeakers. They both were much shaken as they were quickly evicted from the room while the doctor tried unsuccessfully to revive him.

Michael was devastated and went into a depressive grieving for his dad, while Manuela tried to put on a brave face to keep him from having a breakdown. With the help of her husband's brother, Manuela made final arrangements for a wake and burial. With tears in her eyes, she signed off on them with the funeral home.

Michael Sr.'s wake was a somber affair because of its heartrending nature. Family, friends, neighbors and work colleagues surrounded Michael and Manuela with their condolences and love. Michael was very depressed and distraught, and stayed by himself, as many people he didn't know came over to share his grief. They embraced him, telling him his father was a wonderful man, a great friend or a helpful colleague. People told young Michael of how his father helped them. An older woman stopped to tell the son how his dad would fix things for her after her husband died. Michael suddenly felt sweaty and very uncomfortable and had to go to the restroom and wash his face in cold water. He then went outside and breathed in the night's air. After a few minutes, he went back in and was looking at the sign-in book when he overheard his dad's brother talking to someone in a small room nearby.

"Yeah, it was really sad. My brother Michael was killed by that damn drunk on his way to the mall to pick up a computer for his son. It was a surprise for his birthday. He told me the new one had more memory that young people need today. Ironic, isn't it? Doing something nice like that and dying for it."

Michael was stunned. His dad was dead because of him. His grief turned to guilt. He became so upset that he walked home, almost four miles, in the dark. When he got there, he was exhausted and felt sick. He went up to his room and sat on his bed and wept. He kept saying to himself, "It was my fault." He became so agitated that he got up and ended up in the kitchen and made himself a cup of cocoa. He sat with it in the den and turned on the TV. The station was showing a movie with a car chase that ended in a horrible crash. Michael turned the television off and threw away what was left in his cup. He was in a highly emotional state, feeling guilty about not being home when his dad needed him. His father died because of a stupid computer, something Michael would have told his dad he didn't need. If only he had been home instead of on vacation, his father would still be alive.

The front door flew open. Manuela came running in and immediately saw that Michael was in a highly emotional state. She embraced him and held him tightly until he calmed down. When she asked what happened to upset him so much, he told her about overhearing his uncle's conversation and his feeling of guilt for causing his father to die.

Manuela gripped him by the shoulders.

"Son, you are not guilty of anything. Something terrible happened, and the only one who is guilty is the drunk driver who hit your dad's car. I'm so sorry you had to hear about that. Your father asked me what to buy and I suggested it. This was one of those times when a bad thing can unfortunately happen to a good person doing a good deed. None of that is because of you."

For the time Manuela was with Michael, he calmed down. As soon as she left, his mind was focused on his dark thoughts that he was to blame.

Michael and his mom fell on hard times because of Michael Sr.'s tragic death. Michael hung out in his room listening to the radio and still feeling guilty he wasn't home for his father. As he went by Manuela's bedroom at night because he couldn't sleep, he heard her crying softly. Realizing his mom needed him to step up, he tried to comfort her. He also needed to find a way to help with expenses. Despite that life had thrown Michael a terrible curve, his only priority now was to be there for his mom. He had to get through this shattering loss and find a job so he could contribute. During that time of sorrow, Sophia's last letter to him sat unanswered. He put it in his bedroom drawer, not knowing what to say. Maybe he would write her when he felt better.

To pass the time at home, still not dealing well with his father's death, he listened to the records his grandfather gave him on the old vinyl record player his dad bought for him in a secondhand store in New York City. His pet Molly kept him company, seeming to sense Michael's mood. Michael walked her, sometimes for miles, to give her the exercise her breed craved and to escape from the sad reality at home. The long walks not only helped to keep him physically fit, but they also elevated his mood from breathing in the air and seeing people he knew. His friend Don told him about Conti's, an Italian deli that was looking for someone to work part-time. Michael went to Conti's busy store and was immediately embraced by Mrs. Conti, who was aware of the family's loss. She hired him on the spot to help unload deliveries and stock shelves after school. On Saturdays, he could also help deliver groceries with Mr. Conti, who was told not to carry more than small items after he had a hernia operation.

The lifting and carrying heavy items at the store and making deliveries helped to make Michael stronger and more athletic. He also found other odd jobs; babysitting a relative's children, mowing lawns in the spring and summer, and shoveling snow in the winter. When another letter arrived from Sophia, Michael felt so guilty he hadn't responded, he couldn't even bring himself to open it. Manuela noticed what he was doing and suggested it wasn't fair to Sophia to not to write her back. Feeling guilty about it, he sat at his desk and wrote her a letter.

"*Dear Sophia,*

I am so sorry I haven't been in touch, but my father's death has been a terrible blow to my mom and me. We are still dealing with a lot right now and I have no idea what will happen to us.

Thank you for sending the Mass card and your parents for sending flowers for the wake. Please don't feel bad if I don't write you, as things are weird right now.

Your friend, Michael."

Michael addressed the envelope but left it on his father's desk and forgot to mail it for several weeks. Manuela noticed it under some papers and brought it to the post office on her way to work.

Manuela had made the decision to make it her mission to pay off the debts that accumulated from her husband's death. This put extra financial pressure on the two. Manuela listened avidly when her cousin Angela told her that a greeting card company was looking for someone. The applicant would have to be able to create those bright quips, short love poems and clever and funny messages. Angela remembered that Manuela sent her own clever sayings on the back of cards she sent her and other family members. Manuela took Angela's advice and sent samples of the quips she wrote to people. At the same time Manuela was buoyed by the new opportunity to use her creative skills, Michael was given a lift by a kind music teacher. When she heard him sing in an empty classroom, she was very impressed. She had heard what happened to the boy's father and gave him permission to sit in on any music class when he had a free period. It triggered a new passion to learn everything about music and he became a serious student, which improved his ability as a singer.

Another letter came from Sophia, but Michael didn't open it. Sophia reminded him of the happier times he spent in Italy and the painful reality that he wasn't home for his dad when he was needed and maybe could have stopped him from buying the stupid computer.

Chapter 7

BECOMING MICHAEL VENTURA

Manuela was pleasantly surprised to get a call from the greeting card company's creative director to come in for an interview. Thrilled by the opportunity, she quickly went through her past notes to people that she stored in a bedroom drawer and made up a one-page resume and attached a page with ten of her best quips. The human resource department interviewer was disappointed by her lack of professional experience in the greeting card business. Because he liked her offbeat wit and personality, he referred her to the creative director. He also was very impressed by Manuela's witty banter and her amazing ability to quickly come up with clever responses to various greeting card scenarios. It convinced him to hire her.

Manuela's new career challenged her creativity and gave her the ability to receive a decent paycheck. The family's financial prospects were now on the upswing. Seeing his mom so happy gave Michael a new outlook, encouraging him to test his own creative juices. Besides working on his ability to sing the old standards, he penned some song lyrics and then tried his hand at putting them to music, which he composed. He played them for the music teacher, who thought they showed promise. She encouraged him to think about a possible career in music.

The wrongful death lawsuit from the car crash that killed Michael's dad was finally settled after several years of frustrating litigation. It was a new judge assigned to the case who told the attorneys for the insurance company to settle with the aggrieved party or he would impose one. The insurance company then told their attorneys to end their obfuscation and delays. With the settlement, Manuela was finally able to pay off the mortgage on the house and all the accumulated debts. Michael's everyday life quickly became more comfortable, and he was able to quit his job at the store. Now he could concentrate on his music, which became the sole focus outside of his schoolwork.

A neighbor who worked as a DJ at a radio station told Manuela that Michael had serious talent after hearing him. He suggested that she get Michael a voice teacher who could increase his range and smooth out his vocal phrasing. Manuela quickly took his advice and found a voice coach for him. Inspired by the teacher's encouragement, Michael became serious about also playing two musical instruments: the piano and guitar. Manuela was so happy he was interested in pursuing positive things, she bought both instruments for his seventeenth birthday. After asking her neighbor's advice, she also hired another instructor to come once a week.

During his junior year in high school, Michael became more conscious of his physical appearance and started lifting weights. This routine improved his strength as well as sculpted his body into the best shape of his life. He also became intrigued by Aikido, one of the Japanese martial arts, and began watching training videos and practicing the moves in his room. Knowing he needed someone to be an opponent, he asked his friend Don to join him. Within a few weeks, the two friends became pretty good at the moves. However, not being trained in a Dojo or having real opponents made their friendly Aikido matches just two guys playing. The self-taught skill did come in handy a week later, when a group of his friends were playing basketball at a nearby park.

A bunch of older guys in their twenties arrived, and a tall lanky guy who acted as their spokesmen put up his hand to stop play.

"Okay kids, it's time to leave."

Don, who was well over six feet tall, left the court to confront him. "We're almost finished. If you wait over there, we'll be finished in about fifteen."

The spokesman became aggressive and moved to within inches of Don and put his hands on the young boy's chest. "That is not one of the options."

Don took the aggressor's arm and pulled him forward and sent him flying into the chain-link fence. It shocked the older young men to see the kid dispose of their friend so easily. One of the other young men came from the group and looked at Don and the rest of Michael's friends.

"There's no need for that. Look, I know my friend Rick came on too strong, but you guys must have been playing awhile, give us a chance."

Don extended his arms widely, indicating he understood. "We aren't looking to hog the place. Just let us finish this game and we're outta here in a flash."

Rick had picked himself off the ground by the fence, seething with anger at being embarrassed in front of his friends. He started to charge Don, who was still facing away from the fence. Michael saw him out of the corner of his eye and quickly grabbed the guy's wrist and kicked out his back legs as he tried to get by and flipped him onto his back. One of the other older men came over and helped his friend up.

"Cool it, Rick. These kids are almost finished. We'll wait over there."

Somehow, the story of the confrontation in the park got embellished along the way. By the time the story spread at school, Don and Michael had single-handedly taken down a large group of college students. Michael got a kick out of the gossip, but no matter how he tried to set the record straight, the story had taken on a life of its own. The good thing about it was that nobody wanted to mess with either of them. He stopped trying to tell what really happened when several of the popular girls began paying him more attention.

His music teacher arranged for Michael to sing a medley of the old romantic standards at the school's talent recital. After performing two iconic love songs, Michael quickly became even more popular with the girls. He was flattered and liked all the attention. He went out with some of the most attractive and popular girls. After a few weeks of frequent dating, he was exhausted and realized his new social life was a distraction from his real interests.

He backed off from the limelight and focused his energy on two new interests. He wanted to join the wrestling team and became interested in the school's theater group. When the wrestling coach heard Michael was interested, he checked with one of his best student wrestlers about what he knew about the Rasmussen kid. The folklore story about the confrontation in the park made the coach very amenable to having him try out for the team. After being accepted, Michael was energized by the physical training routine and the challenge of competing. He quickly became an outstanding wrestler and all-city finalist in his senior year.

During auditions for the theater program, Michael's natural acting ability caught the attention of the school's theater coach and Vanessa Fielding, the theater group's beautiful leading lady.

Michael's new status at school attracted the attention of the popular cliques. He was accepted by the guys for his athletic ability and found attractive to the girls for his good looks and affable personality. His ability to sing those romantic old love songs didn't hurt as it attracted more girls. Michael started to enjoy his popularity a little too much and found himself taking advantage of it by having sex with several more than willing seniors. He was also invited to join several of the popular groups rumored to hold great drinking parties. He drank so much at one party that he came home so drunk he threw up in the foyer on the stairs but continued up to his room and collapsed on his bed. In the morning, Manuela was so angry at him for leaving his mess on the new carpet, she shook him until he opened his bleary eyes. She made him throw up again by giving him an awful drink made with a sports drink, a raw egg and Pepto-Bismol. Two weeks later, Michael was invited to one of the more raucous parties with free-flowing alcohol and drugs. This time, he woke up in a bedroom at the party. He was in his underwear, had a terrible hangover and two drunken girls lay next to him in bed. When he staggered in at two am, Manuela was waiting and told him in a very angry tone that she was ashamed of him and that his dad would have been so disappointed in his bad behavior. Being reminded about what his father would think of him was a powerful wake-up call.

The next evening, a contrite son told his mom he felt terrible about his bad behavior, and he promised that he had sworn off the party scene. When Michael was next invited to a party, he begged off, saying that he was too busy and had to practice his musical instruments and make more time for his vocal coach. Michael became determined to focus on what was important in his life: finding a nice steady girlfriend with similar interests and honoring his dad's memory by being a good person like him.

Later that term, Michael did have a secret girlfriend he didn't tell anyone about at school. He was dating Vanessa Fielding, everybody's fantasy girl. She represented the trifecta of a girlfriend: hot, talented and smart. Michael and Vanessa had decided they didn't need the angst of school gossip and petty jealousy. Their relationship was initially based on their mutual respect for each other's talents as well as their physical attraction to the other. Vanessa had more experience in acting and was happy to share what she had learned taking lessons since she was six years old. Michael shared what he learned from his voice coach. Despite Michael's recent short encounters with girls at wild parties, Vanessa was more sexually experienced than Michael. She was more than ready to share it with him but decided to go slow. She was concerned it might affect their friendship and when they had to perform together. Michael was totally enamored with Vanessa and was not planning to take a vow of celibacy. However, he was also concerned that if he tried to get too amorous, it might affect their growing personal friendship. Because both wanted to perform together, their relationship became a sexually charged standoff while a great friendship grew out of it.

In Michael's senior year everything began to change rapidly for both. The high school theater group decided to stage the iconic rock-'n'-roll musical *Bye Bye Birdie*. Michael was encouraged by the theater's new moderator, who heard him sing offstage, to try out. Vanessa and many of his theater mates wanted him for the Conrad Birdie part. He reluctantly auditioned and was given the role. When Vanessa was given the part of Kim McAfee, who was the object of Birdie's attention, he was happy that he had tried out. Michael began slowly to relate to the character's feeling of celebrity and the character's Elvis-like control of the audience. Michael studied the film version of the play over and over until he became the fascinating fictional character. He also watched Elvis Presley's movies to see the iconic rock-'n'-roll idol's vocal delivery and physical gyrations, which made girls and women swoon and scream when he sang. The fact that his character was to kiss Vanessa, who was playing Kim, made doing the role a double pleasure.

Vanessa's father, Bart Fielding. attended the performance with his wife, Joan, to see his talented daughter. He was also interested in seeing the boy that she was dating as well. Vanessa had told her dad how talented Michael was at singing and acting. As a top agent for television projects, he was always interested in finding and developing new talent. What made Bart very interested was that his opinionated and accomplished daughter never thought anyone was ever good, even the professionals his highly respected agency represented. He was curious to see why his critical daughter thought her friend was so uniquely talented.

When Michael came on stage opening night, the audience was totally mesmerized as he became the character of Birdie. The musical was composed for the stage by Charles Strauss, with the lyrics by Lee Adams. The book was influenced by Elvis Presley's energetic performances and his effect on audiences. Michael had mastered the rock-star singing style, and his performance energized the other actors. in their roles. In his duet with Vanessa, Michael nailed it as he sang Birdie's big number, "Honestly Sincere." He knocked it out of the park with Vanessa with his rendition of "A Lot of Livin' to Do."

While the boys in the audience checked out Vanessa, Michael's personal good looks and singing ability were attracting the girls. Their audible reactions were contagious and spread to others. Bart Fielding, sitting and observing, couldn't help but notice. Joan Fielding even turned to her husband and gave him a "What's that all about?" look.

When the play ended, the audience gave the cast a standing ovation. When Michael individually took his bow, the response was thunderous. Bart saw that his daughter Vanessa had an eye for discovering talent, as Michael's performance had reprised the Conrad Birdie character with dead-on accuracy. After the final curtain, Bart and Joan went backstage to bring their daughter flowers and meet Michael. They found the two together very excited by the audience's reaction. Bart spoke to Michael while Joan congratulated Vanessa. He found the talented teen to be modest, respectful and thoughtful. He gave him his business card and told Michael to call, and he'd set up a meeting with the firm's top talent agent, Mary McDaniel. While Bart went over to hug and praise his daughter, Joan came over to congratulate Michael and tell him she thought his performance was special. She then pointedly asked Michael to compare his onstage chemistry with the character Kim with his offstage social relationship with Vanessa. Michael became flustered by the question as she waited patiently to hear his reply.

"Your daughter is an amazing talent and an amazing person. She's talented and beautiful like Kim."

"I agree. She has a great future ahead of her, don't you think?"

"Of course. You and Mr. Fielding have raised a terrific person. Everybody admires her."

Joan Fielding gave Michael an appraising once-over. "Well, good luck to you, Michael. You both have great careers ahead of you, so it's important for both of you to stay safe and not take risks that could adversely affect your futures."

After she left, Michael wondered what the conversation with Vanessa's mother was about. He thought about asking Vanessa but was quickly being surrounded by the rest of the cast who wanted to celebrate.

Within a few days of calling Mr. Fielding, Michael had a meeting at his agency. Mary McDaniel was more than ready to listen to the handsome, well-built 18-year-old. A talented singer who could act and play the piano and guitar and was recommended by Bart Fielding was a find. After a sit-down discussion with Michael, Mary was very impressed with his knowledge of music. He displayed unusual insight for an 18-year-old. Mary was surprised by Michael's awareness of how music influenced culture and cultural shifts influenced music. Michael was also able to speak informatively about the historic changes caused by technology and recent changes that were happening in the music business itself. As Mary listened to him sing, that brought back memories of the great singing stars that made the old songs famous—a genre that she had personally loved. Michael's vocal range and unique phrasing of the old standards convinced her there was something special about the young man. After the audition, Mary immediately called Chris Manning, one of the top music producers, who agreed to listen to him the next week.

Michael came into the recording studio, which was well equipped for auditions. After listening to him, Chris agreed the young man had talent, but was concerned about the marketability of someone who sang a genre made up of old standards and love songs. Michael told him that he could also sing current pop or soft rock. He reminded the producer that there was a treasure trove of some of the best music from the past missing in the music business because everyone else was focusing on the new trends. He believed that tapping into an underserved market was a good business marketing strategy. Chris had to admire Michael's analysis. He thought to himself that in most business ventures, Michael would have been spot on, but this was the music business. He asked Michael to sing another song, one of his personal favorites. Michael thought for a moment about the challenge and said okay.

"If it's all right with you, I'll sing 'All I do is Dream of You.' It's an old love song that was first published in 1934 and was a fan favorite when performed in the great musical movie

Singing in the Rain by Debbie Reynolds, and later became popular with many male and female singers."

"Great. Let's see what you got."

Now the producer became fully engaged in an unusual audition strategy. He instructed the sound engineer to have the speakers connect through the office sound system. Then he opened the blinds that usually blocked the office staff from seeing the auditions. Chris then asked his assistant to go around the office and let the staff know that a new young talent was auditioning and would like their personal reaction. Michael had selected a song which in some ways was dangerous. His rendition would be compared with the original stars who sang it. When he began singing, Chris was impressed by his command of the material, his vocal quality and his relaxed delivery. He again thought that while this kid had potential, Chris had the same reservation. Would Michael's rendition stand up against the many pros who made it a hit song?

When he turned to talk to the sound man, a crowd of women from the office were at the viewing window, wanting a glimpse of the singer. Bart told the person standing in the back to open the door and let in whoever wanted to meet Michael as he finished. Several women came in and rushed up to Michael, some taking his arm and telling him that he was terrific. One of the normally laid-back senior staff women was gushing to Michael about his voice and phrasing. This highly respected employee started to hug Michael like was her son. Chris observed as two younger female interns came over to ask for his autograph. While Michael accommodated them, they were touching his arm and shoulder. As one of them left, she planted a quick kiss on his cheek. Chris watched how well Michael interacted with each one, and he kept nodding his head, amazed by the reaction in the office. He said to himself, "Mary may be right about this kid."

After he discussed it with several of his staff for their opinion, Chris decided to get Michael a test gig. There was a small club named Frankie's, aptly named after the owner's singing idol in the old days. It was frequented by well-to-do customers, many of them in the entertainment business. He thought if Michael could please the owner, Frank DeCicco, and his crowd, the kid might be someone to develop. Chris suggested that Michael reprise the song he sang at his office, as it seemed to cause a stir with a staff that was usually cynical when he auditioned singers. He suggested that Michael prepare to perform three more of his favorite songs, just in case. Michael quickly agreed because he had been singing that standard and knew he could easily be ready to sing three others.

When he met with Vanessa the next day to tell her the news, she was very excited for him. She had been working with Mary McDaniel for a year and trusted her judgement. The agent had arranged for her to develop her dancing skills and found a special voice coach to her get ready for a Broadway musical career. Mary had secured Vanessa a place at the Strasberg acting studio after she graduated high school, so she could also become a serious actor in film or television. Michael became excited for Vanessa. They both talked about their future in entertainment like it was already a foregone fact.

When they came back to reality, Vanessa turned to Michael and suggested they go to Frankie's to check out the place. At first, he was hesitant because Chris hadn't arranged it. Vanessa was very persuasive, pointing out Michael would get to know the physical layout and be better prepared. This way there wouldn't be any surprises when he went to rehearse the afternoon of the performance. Michael had to agree that Vanessa was right. The last thing he wanted was to look foolish on one of the most important days of his life.

As he walked Vanessa home, the talented teens held hands,

fantasizing about their showbiz futures. When they arrived, her dad's car wasn't there. Michael asked if her father was away.

Vanessa at first looked puzzled, then her face lit up. "I remember now. My dad told me they had this reception for an important agency client in the city. He and my mom were going to stay over at the company's apartment."

Michael looked concerned. "You okay staying by yourself?"

"Why? Would you like to keep me company?"

"Ah...err...sure, if it's okay with you."

"It'd be nice to have company. I'd feel safer with you in the house, that's for sure."

"Of course. I'll be like your bodyguard."

Vanessa smiled teasingly. "The question is...do I need someone to guard my body from the bodyguard?"

Michael blushed and then teased back. "Do you want someone to protect your body from your bodyguard?"

"Hmm...don't think I do."

Michael tightened his grip on her hand. "Then I promise to guard it as closely as you want me to."

The two went into the house, which was empty except for the family cat lying on the living room couch and ignoring them. When Vanessa said she was going heat up some leftovers, Michael asked to use the phone.

"It's over there on the wall."

"I'll just call my mom, so she doesn't worry."

"Hi...I'm going to stay with a friend tonight. I'll see you in the morning."

"Give Vanessa my best...be safe."

As he hung up, Michael shook his head and smiled, as he was surprised that his mother was on to him. He commented at the phone as he placed it back on the wall

"Mother, you are a piece of work."

Michael watched Vanessa prepare the meal with admiration. She got a kick out of what his mother said.

"Do you think it's possible our mothers are in touch with each other?"

"Let's hope not!"

After they ate all the leftover meatloaf and mashed potatoes in the refrigerator, Vanessa went to the wine rack and selected a red wine. As she poured it, Michael put up his hand.

"Not for me! My grandfather owns a winery in Italy, so I tried drinking wine as a kid. I didn't like it."

"I know what you're saying. Trust me, it's worth a try now that you're older. Besides, this is an expensive Merlot my dad buys by the case."

"Okay, I'm game if you are. Let's give it a try."

As the two sipped the expensive wine, Michael had to agree, it was very good. By the time the two finished the bottle, they were a little high and their inhibitions were getting a little low. The wine made Vanessa a little feisty as she showed Michael her room and pointed to the bed.

"I was thinking it might be safer for me if you stay with me here."

Michael reflected a slight hesitancy. Vanessa reacted.

"You look uncomfortable."

"I didn't expect...I'm sorry but I don't have any protection with me."

"Not a problem. After my mom saw you play Birdie and made all those girls faint and she already knew we were dating, she asked my doctor to put me on the pill. Wait a minute, I just remembered; she thought of everything."

When Vanessa left the room, Michael felt embarrassed, feeling like an unsophisticated jerk. As she came back into the room, Vanessa tossed him a packet of condoms.

"This is the other thing that my mom said I should get from her drawer if I ever needed to."

Michael couldn't help smiling, then a thought flashed in

his memory.

"When you said that, it made me think of that song from that old movie *Gigi* I saw on TCM."

"Really? *Gigi*? I don't get it. Why?"

Michael stared singing "*Thank heaven for little girls,*" mimicking Maurice Chevalier

"You saying I grew up in the most delightful way?"

"You did, but tonight our mothers made me want to rewrite the lines... Thank heaven for thoughtful mothers. They do things in the most delightful way."

Vanessa laughed at Michael's new lyric. "You're a little kooky...but you are a talented kook."

"Now I understand why your mom asked about our chemistry in *Birdie*, and all the precautionary things she provided. It's pretty cool when you think about it."

"I agree, but they're a little spooky too. By the way, I loved the way you sang that line from *Gigi*. You may be really good at doing other people's voices, so if your singing career doesn't work out, you have a backup."

"I'll keep that in mind."

"Come! Let's go take a shower. You said I grew up in the most delightful way. I want to see how this Rasmussen boy grew up."

Vanessa took Michael by the hand and the two friends went into the bathroom and closed the door.

When Michael woke up, he was a little groggy from the evening's drinking and very exhausted from being attentive to Vanessa's body. As he looked over at her naked back, he couldn't help being turned on and began kissing her neck, which awakened the sleeping beauty.

"Michael...did I fall asleep while you were still pleasuring me?"

"No, it's really morning. I just woke up myself but couldn't resist kissing your beautiful neck. Last night, I really liked kissing all of you."

"And I liked you kissing all of me."

"You know, I always loved the way you looked, talked, and sang...now I also love the way you feel, smell and taste."

"Wait one minute! Are you saying you're a cannibal and want to eat me after you have your way with me?"

Michael was momentarily speechless and before he could think of a comeback, the alarm clock started ringing loudly. As Vanessa shut it off, she smiled, knowing he was stumped for a reply.

"Sorry, Michael, no time for an answer. We have to clean up fast. They probably got up at are on the way home."

The two showered and dressed quickly and cleaned up the bedroom and the kitchen. As Vanessa practically pushed him out the door, Michael said he'd pick her up to go to Frankie's at one o'clock. Vanessa watched as Michael walked quickly down the street and smiled, thinking about him being saved by the bell.

As Michael started to jog home, he was still trying to come with a smart quip for Vanessa when he spotted Bart Fielding's car turning into the street to their house. He quickly ducked behind a hedge. After they passed, he sprinted the rest of the way until he was in the door.

Manuela heard him enter and came out of the kitchen. "I made breakfast."

"I could eat."

"How did the sleepover go?"

"Great. Vanessa cooked; we talked a lot. I wanted her to be protected while her parents were in New York City."

"Having protection is a good thing. I'm sure her parents would agree."

Michael made a low "*grr*," as he stared at Manuela realizing what protection she was talking about. Manuela decided to change the conversation.

"What's on your docket today, my talented son?"

"I have that audition next week, so I'm going to check out the place this afternoon."

"Want me to go with you?"

"Vanessa said she would, and I need to borrow the car."

"That's okay. Let's eat now. I'm very hungry. You'll have plenty of time to get ready after."

While they ate, Manuela subtly tried to find out more about her son's sleepover. Michael was onto her probing questions and only gave up G-rated information.

As Michael left with her car keys, looking spiffy in a white turtleneck and his new blue jacket, Manuela smiled broadly, seeing that he was so grown up.

When Michael arrived at the Fielding house, he was greeted at the door by Vanessa's mother, who invited him to come in.

"Michael, you look very nice. Vanessa tells me you are both going to scope out Frankie's for your first professional performance."

"She suggested it would be good to know the lay of the land, so to speak."

"Makes sense. You both are coming back after you check out the place. I have to plan dinner."

"Probably. I have to get home to rehearse."

Vanessa came into the vestibule and looked at the two talking with curiosity.

"I'm ready to go. You two finished?"

"Michael's planning to rehearse later, so I'll plan that you'll have dinner with us. You can catch me up on how it went."

"Okay."

Vanessa grabbed Michael's arm and ushered him out of the house. As they hit the sidewalk, Vanessa looked seriously at Michael.

"Did she say anything to you about last night?"

"No. Just talked about the dinner thing."

"I was afraid she was going to grill you."

Michael turned to her with a serious straight face. "Why would your mom want to do that? Is she a cannibal?"

Vanessa laughed and pushed him hard in his arm. "You make any cheesier jokes like that, and I'll cook you myself."

"I'm cooked every time I think about last night."

Vanessa tried to control herself from reacting. "Stop it. We have an important mission to do. I don't want to be distracted by your crazy jokes, and like that Las Vegas saying, 'What happens in my bedroom, should be left in my bedroom.'"

"Oh. I almost forgot—a cannibal in some situations should eat before, not after."

Vanessa looked at Michael, confused for a minute as she tried to understand, then burst out laughing and punched his arm. "You're bad!"

Michael made out she had hurt him but couldn't stop smiling.

Vanessa reached over and rubbed Michael's shoulder gently as they drove. "Michael, I think you and I should think about where our relationship is heading."

Michael nodded but kept his eyes on the road. "Personally, I like the way it's going. What are you thinking?"

"We are really great together, but we are both heading toward show biz careers. That means we'll probably end up in different places. I think we should enjoy what time we have together but recognize the reality that our careers will separate us. This way neither of us will get hurt and we'll always be good friends."

"Wow, that's pretty deep stuff. You're right about one thing you said, I will never want to hurt you. So, if that other thing happens, you have to be the one to tell me it's time to say goodbye."

Michael reached over to touch Vanessa's cheek. They both

sat in silence until they arrived at Frankie's. As they walked from the parking lot, where there were only two cars, Michael looked at Vanessa and shrugged.

"This place probably doesn't get customers during the day. We should be able to check out the stage without any trouble."

Michael went to open the entrance door, but it was locked. He began knocking hard. Finally, the door opened, and a very large man answered.

"What do ya want, kid?

"Hi, I'm Michael Rasmussen. I'm singing here next week-end and I wanted to just check out the facilities. This is my friend, Vanessa."

"Is this a joke?"

"No, sometimes I make them... Wait, you're serious? My name is Michael Rasmussen, and I'm really supposed to sing here. Call Chris Manning, he booked me."

The big man shook his head in disbelief. "Wait here. I have to check with the boss."

The door slammed shut, and Vanessa took his elbow. "Did you say something about not having trouble?"

Michael shrugged. The two waited in an awkward silence for five minutes until the door finally opened. The big man waved them in.

"Please come in. Mr. Manning didn't tell the boss you were so young. People who entertain here usually are old enough to drink. I'm Matt."

"You do know, Matt, that people our age do drink...but I understand about the legal thing, so I promise that I will only have water or a soft drink when I'm here to perform."

Matt chuckled. "You're okay, kid. Welcome to the joint. Check out any-thing, but be fast; the musicians are coming soon, and they'll be rehearsing on the stage."

Michael and Vanessa were given the tour and checked out the stage and the microphone and sound equipment. They even met the owner, Frank DeCicco, who scratched his head as he looked Michael in the eye.

"Hey Michael...not for nothin'...you really are a singer, right? Manning isn't screwing with us?"

Michael smiled and looked him in the eye. "Mr. DeCicco, I am a singer and Chris is not screwing with you! Please thank Matt for the tour. See you both next week."

Frankie looked at Michael quizzically then smiled admiringly. "Then I look forward to your performing here."

Michael shook his hand and escorted Vanessa out of the club. When they were outside, he turned to Vanessa.

"I hope this age thing doesn't mess me up."

"Don't worry about it. You are so talented they'll get over it when you sell out stadiums."

"From your lips to God's ears...my dad's mother used to say that."

Vanessa kissed Michael sweetly on the lips. "And my lips wanted to do that."

"If you keep doing that, I'll never get you home. I promised your mom."

Michael kept his promise and rehearsed that week and was ready for his big break.

On the night of his debut at Frankie's, Michael was stoked; excited to be finally singing as a professional and getting paid five hundred dollars. The place was packed by the time the comedian had finished his routine and riffed a bit with the audience. As the headliner that night, the pressure was on Michael to deliver for the customers who were paying big bucks for their night out. When Michael was introduced, many did a double take, wondering why Frankie would book such a young person since the place had a reputation for attracting an older, more sophisticated crowd. Bart Fielding was there with Joan and Vanessa. Chris Manning brought his assistant. Manuela came with her Creative Director who was curious about his favorite worker's talented offspring. There was a distinguished, well-dressed man sitting at a back table who sat up when he saw Michael come out.

As the band started playing the music for "All I do is Dream of You," the selection that Chris Manning suggested, Michael picked up the microphone and jumped off the stage and started singing to the customers up close at their tables. Everyone stopped chattering and paid attention to the young singer whose voice and audience-friendly style immediately caught their attention, especially the women who loved it when he came to their tables.

Michael's voice and manner immediately mesmerized the women and impressed the men. He was again spot-on in his interpretation and delivery and his choice to sing the old hit songs was perfect for that audience. What was most engaging for his audience was his accessibility by coming and singing to them in a very personal way.

The audience applauded loudly and asked him to sing more songs. He obliged with a medley of three songs from the time of the crooners. One was from Frank Sinatra, "The Way You Look Tonight." After he finished, Frankie DiCecco looked over from his front-row table and nodded to Michael his approval. Michael moved quickly, signaling the bandleader, and followed up with A Dean Martin hit, "That's Amore." As a final song, he sang his buoyant interpretation of "Catch A Falling Star," a favorite by Perry Como. At times, he would look over at Vanessa for her reaction and she would nod her approval. The audience loved the upbeat finish, many forgetting their food and drinks while he was performing.

After taking a bow and thanking the audience, he went off the stage and into the small dressing room, sat down and let out a big sigh of relief. There was a knock at the door and a distinguished, well-dressed, gray-haired man asked if he could come in. Michael nodded and ushered him in.

"Hi, Michael. My name is Gerry Needham. I wanted to come back and congratulate you on a truly wonderful performance."

"Thank you. The audience was so great. I was so grateful for their warm reception."

"That's because you deserved it, young man. Here's my card. You'll see that I'm a concert manager and would love to talk to you when you have time. My expertise is in arranging tours for singers who can command an audience and I have a feeling you will be a natural. I know Chris booked you here so I don't want to interfere with another person's talent, but Chris is a studio recording producer so I think we could all work together if you are willing."

Michael didn't know what to say but then remembered he had an agent. "Mary McDaniel is representing me. Maybe we could meet with her and Chris and sort this out."

Gerry smiled broadly and put his on Michael's shoulder. "You're not only talented; you are a pretty smart guy for your age. That's an excellent idea. I know Mary very well. I'll give her a call."

A meeting was arranged for the next week and an agreement was made between all the interested parties.

After much discussion about giving him a stage name, Michael spoke up, not liking some of the bizarre names being suggested.

"It should be Michael Ventura since it was my grandfather who inspired me to sing."

On reflection, all the advisors thought it was a brilliant solution. Their young singer could follow in the footsteps of other singers of the old standards from an Italian American heritage: Frank Sinatra (Francis Sinatra), Perry Como (Pierino Como), Tony Bennett (Anthony Benedetto) and Dean Martin (Dino Crocetti).

Gerry Needham agreed and then suggested Michael develop his own signature stage outfit for performing in concerts. As an example, he took out a sketch that his sister did for Michael. Rose Needham was a well-known Broadway costume designer who had attended Frankie's with her brother. It was a sketch of Michael dressed in dark blue trousers, a white turtleneck shirt with a blue cashmere sweater. Rose thought something classic but not formal would suit Michael's youth, persona, and casual performance style.

Michael took one quick look.

"Please tell your sister, Rose, that I love it."

And a star named Michael Ventura was born.

Chapter 8

A RISING STAR

Within three years, Michael Ventura became a very popular recording artist who performed at concerts all over the US, Canada, Great Britain, Ireland, Europe and Australia. His fan-friendly performances became a big hit. He enjoyed going into the audience and frequently invited someone who wanted to sing to join him on stage, which always made the concert's security people on edge. Touring became his life and everything else that had been important began to fade. The touring made the recording albums sell and the albums brought people to the concerts. Michael was energized by the synergy, especially the warm audience reception. He enjoyed the thunderous applause, screams and even the occasional sexual invitation or a jealous angry reaction of an exuberant fan's male companion. Each concert presented a new challenge for the security people, who were always on edge if he decided to leave the stage and go into the audience to get and give hugs.

Only his telephone talks with his mom, grandfather and Vanessa connected him to his past. His previous childhood visits to his grandfather's winery in Italy became part of a forgotten time, as his world now revolved around the next performance or recording time. Michael and his manager, Gerry Needham, had formed a close friendship as well as a professional relationship. Gerry thought of Michael as a son he never had and often flew to see him while on tour and have dinner. He liked taking his young star to see the attractions in the cities they played. Michael's rising popularity in the states kept him hopping from city to city. Bookings came in from NYC to Chicago to LA, and most cities in between with large enough indoor arenas and auditoriums. As he traveled, he added fans that bought his albums. Several of the diehard fans formed clubs and looked forward to his television appearances and promotional interviews. Michael's relaxed style of speaking freely and his affable, self-deprecating personality made him a favorite celebrity to interview. He loved to joke around with the other guests and was open to their pulling his chain about his love song genre at his young age. His popularity kept him constantly on the road, making it difficult to spend time with his friends and family.

Though Michael and Vanessa met occasionally in hotel rooms to renew their passionate relationship, they were more often separated by their careers. While he was touring in Europe and Australia, Vanessa was the featured singer on a cruise ship. While he was recording an album in a NYC studio, Vanessa scored a recurring part in a television series that was shot in LA. They tried to talk regularly on the phone but they both sensed their career realities had taken a toll on their relationship.

The "other shoe" fell when Michael called her on Valentine's Day.

"Vanessa, Happy Valentine's Day. Hope you received the flowers. I have some good news. I'll be coming to LA in April for a big fundraiser concert at the Hollywood Bowl."

There was prolonged silence at the other end of the call.

"Vanessa?"

"Michael...I'm sorry you have to hear about it this way. It's that thing we talked about. I met someone three months ago and I moved in with Jeff last week. He's really a great guy. Please know, I will always treasure you as my best friend. I hope you can forgive me."

"Whoa. Didn't expect that! I know we talked about this a long time ago... Can I call you back after I process this?"

"Of course, but please remember I care deeply about you. Jeff and I both would like you in our lives."

Michael thought about the upsetting conversation for a week before calling Vanessa. He invited her and Jeff to be his guests at the concert. Vanessa was so happy to hear from him, she cried on the phone and said they would be proud to come and would give a generous donation at the fundraiser. He put down the phone slowly and let out a big sigh. Michael felt distraught about losing his first real love but happy he made the call. He owed it to Vanessa to meet and check out her new guy.

When Michael performed in LA, he went to a luncheon the day after the concert with Vanessa and her new boyfriend, Jeff Brook. After a slightly awkward introduction, he and Jeff took measure of each other and had a polite conversation. Both expressed their admiration for Vanessa's exceptional talent and special qualities. She felt embarrassed by their appreciation of her and just hoped they would be good friends. By the end of lunch, Jeff had relaxed his concerns that Michael would attempt to mess up his relationship with Vanessa. The three parted as friends of a sort and Michael promised to call when he came to LA. As Michael sat in his chauffeured town car, he let out a big sigh and said a loud "Shit!" The driver sat up and looked at Michael in the rearview mirror. His passenger looked lost, as if someone he cared about had just died.

As the years flew by, Michael's passion for music consumed him, and because of his popularity, he toured extensively to sold-out large venues. When not on the road, he spent a great deal of time in the recording studio making albums of the old standards and a few new ones. Michael made it a point to not get involved with amorous fans like many of his celebrity predecessors did. While he went on occasional dates with women in the business, they were often arranged by his label's publicity staff or Billy, his road manager. Michael enjoyed the female company and an occasional fling but had not found an emotional connection with anyone. He did have other friends who paired him with several interesting and accomplished women, but no one so far could replace the void of losing Vanessa.

Manuela was busy in her own career writing clever poems and sayings for the greeting card company. For a short time, she and her boss would have dinner together until the company's CEO had a talk with him about dating subordinates. These corporate policy concerns triggered the decision to have Manuela arrange to largely work remotely. This remote work assignment gave her the ability to finally visit her dad in Italy and two of her best friends from high school more often.

Michael was now in such high demand that Aurelio, who avidly followed his grandson's career, had to go to see him during a concert he gave in Rome. Michael enjoyed their visit and thanked his grandfather from the stage for his encouragement. One of the songs he performed was a favorite of Aurelio's.

When Michael was twenty-four, thousands of his Italian fans came to his summer concert in Milan, Italy. After a sold-out Friday performance, he decided to surprise his grandfather and travel by helicopter so he could be back for his highly anticipated Saturday evening concert with one of Italy's top female artists.

Aurelio was having a late snack when he heard a helicopter as it came closer to his property. He wondered why someone was flying so low in such a rural area. When it got louder and was hovering by his back field, he went out to investigate just as it descended and landed next to his vegetable garden. He ran over as the blades stopped whirring to confront the intruder. When Michael jumped down, Aurelio was totally stunned and immediately rushed to greet him.

"Michael! What a wonderful surprise. Come into my house and bring your wonderful pilot that brought you to visit me."

While the pilot enjoyed the snacks that Aurelio served, Michael and Aurelio had a wonderful visit. Michael told him about his adventures while touring and Aurelio brought Michael up to date on the winery's situation. As they reminisced about past visits to the Ventura winery, Aurelio remembered Michael visiting when he was a young boy.

"I remember as if it were yesterday, you first came when you were only three years old."

"That I don't really remember. When I was ten, I do remember you bringing me to visit Pietro and learning about winemaking and exploring your vineyards and meeting my friend Sophia. How is she anyway?"

"Why don't you call the Mariano's before it gets too late and talk to her? She always asks me about you when she visits."

"Wow! That would be a blast from the past, but I'm afraid Sophia may not want to hear from me. I was a terrible friend after my dad died. Sophia wrote a few letters. I finally wrote one telling her I was not functioning very well. Then life took me in a new direction. What must she think of me?"

"Call her and find out."

"You're right. I'll give it a try."

Michael dialed and Maria Mariano answered.

"Hi, Mrs. Mariano, this is Michael. I'm at my grandfather's

house and wondered if I could speak to Sophia."

"Michael, how wonderful to hear your voice! We all are so proud of your success. It's been such a long time. I'm sorry, but Sophia went with her girlfriends to Sabaudia to enjoy the beach and have some fun after she graduated college."

"A college graduate! I'm so happy for her. I hope she is having a good time. Give her my best when she returns."

"Will you be staying with Aurelio?"

"I have to fly back in the morning to Milan, for a concert."

"Ah...you're the helicopter sound we heard."

"Afraid so. Well, give your husband my regards. I think when we were kids that Sophia and I made him a little crazy."

"Francesco grew up only with brothers. I don't think he understood his young daughter. I will tell him you called. Please give Manuela a big hug for us. We'd love to see her again."

"I'll tell her. Goodbye."

After hanging up, Michael shrugged, realizing Sophia and he had moved on with their lives. He turned to Aurelio.

"Sophia is celebrating with her friends in Sabaudia. I'm so happy to hear she graduated from college. She was always a smart kid. If it's okay with you, we'll stay over and leave in the morning. I don't like flying in a chopper in the dark."

"Casa mia é casa tua." (My house is your house.)

"Nothing would make me happier than to make coffee and breakfast for you and your pilot."

Aurelio came over to his grandson and gave him a hug and kisses on both cheeks. Michael took him by the shoulders.

"How about sharing a bottle of Ventura wine to celebrate?"

"I have a special one saved just for this occasion."

Aurelio invited Pietro to join Michael and Phil, his pilot, and they ended up finishing off two bottles of his best vintage wine, his best provolone cheese and all his homemade bread. They all slept well. Aurelio was up early to make his guests a special breakfast. After an emotional goodbye with Michael and a big hug from the pilot, Aurelio watched them as they made their way to the helicopter. As they took off, Aurelio waved furiously then wiped the tears from his eyes. Pietro, who had stayed over, put his arm around Aurelio.

"It's wonderful to see Michael all grown up and such a successful man. You should be proud for inspiring him."

Wiping his eyes, Aurelio turned to his old friend. "He is a wonderful young man, isn't he?"

Michael's last concert in Milan was a big hit and the promoter asked if he would come back soon. He promised to talk to Gerry and return as soon as his schedule allowed. When Michael finished the tour in London, he anxiously called his mom to see how his pet Molly was doing. When he last called from Milan, Manuela told him she was failing. Molly was now over sixteen years old well past her breed's normal life span.

"I'm sorry Michael, but Molly passed a few days ago and I didn't call because you were performing, and I was concerned it would affect your concert in London. I took a paw print and saved her tag for you then had our wonderful pet buried in the woods behind your house. I was so upset after, I did something a little crazy. I searched and tracked down one of the puppies that came from her offspring's litter. That would make her Molly's great grand dog. I checked her out at an onsite meeting with the AKC breeder. DeeDee was being playful and loving to a group of children. The woman who managed the place said the three-year-old DeeDee wasn't up to the breed's standard length for showing so they would sell her, and I'd get the pet in two days. They named her DeeDee after some Irish relative. If you like, we can rename her as she is still young and will adjust if you prefer a different name."

Michael was still processing the bad news about his beloved pet Molly while his mom was talking.

"Mom, please stop. I don't know how I feel about replacing

Molly so soon."

"I'll tell you what. Since I will take care of any pet because of your travel requirements, I'll take her in. When you're back, you can decide to take her or not, or if you want us to have shared custody, that will be okay too."

"Mom, you should be a diplomat. That sounds like something that King Solomon guy would have come up with. I can't argue with your reasoning, but the news about Molly is too fresh. So I'll look forward to seeing both of you in two weeks."

Manuela smiled as she hung up the phone.

"Isn't that something? My famous son thinks I'm like King Solomon. I could get used to that."

Chapter 9

FINDING LOVE

At his next performance in Madison Square Garden, Michael shared with the audience about losing Molly, who was his precious childhood pet. He then performed an emotional interpretation of the song "Smile" in her memory. He told them that Nat King Cole recorded it in 1954, though the music was composed originally for a Charlie Chaplin film in 1936. As Michael sang a heartrending rendition of this old classic, Louisa Romano, a violinist in the orchestra, teared up. When he left the stage, he passed her and she saw that he was sad. She let out a sigh, feeling sad herself that he had lost his pet. She followed him with her eyes as he came from the stage to leave and encountered an emotional woman who spontaneously wanted to hug him as he passed her by. This triggered her jealous boyfriend to physically attack him, sucker-punching him as passed. Michael had to wrestle him to the ground before the concert security people took over. Louisa Romano became so upset, she decided on the spot to do something about Michael's dilemma.

Louisa got up the courage and intercepted Michael the next day as he came to prep for the evening.

"Mr. Ventura. My name is Louisa Romano. I play the violin in the touring orchestra. I saw what happened yesterday and know it's something you've had to deal with on occasion. If you think it would help, I could act as your faux girlfriend and discourage fans from causing an awkward situation like what just happened. I think this woman was just emotionally caught up in your loss of Molly and then you sang that beautiful sad song. To be honest, I know the feeling, because I teared up and wanted to hug you myself."

Michael smiled as he looked at the beautiful young woman, with green eyes like his mom, who was so sincere he wanted to hug her on the spot. He resisted as his security guys were watching closely and would tease him for being a sentimental softy.

"Louisa, you are very sweet and kind to offer to do that, and I think you are right about the woman was emotional and not sexual. It was her boyfriend who had the problem, since I made no moves that warranted his angry reaction. Just know, I am somewhat trained to deal with this possibility and my security men are usually right there. I wouldn't want you to have to deal with a potentially dangerous encounter like that."

Michael then took Louisa by the elbow. "Incidentally, I did know your name because I asked who you were when I heard you rehearse your solo the other day. You are a very talented musician. I know because I wish I could play the guitar and piano half as well as you play your violin."

Louisa blushed. "Thank you, Mr. Ventura. You are always so nice to all of us, it makes me proud to be part of your tour."

"Please, call me Michael, and thank you. I appreciate that you all do your best to make the concerts a success. I also want you to know your suggestion has merit. It's the security issues for you I would be concerned about."

Michael gave Louisa a quick cheek hug, making her blush again.

"I will talk to my manager about your suggestion."

When Michael ran Louisa's suggestion past Gerry, his manager, he was surprised by Gerry's quick reaction. He thought it was brilliant and was sure security would be able to keep the young woman safe. Michael promised he'd think about it. When a similar situation with a jealous husband happened on the weekend's concert in Chicago, he agreed to try the arrangement if it didn't put Louisa in danger.

Michael played the fake dating game as an experiment at first to keep his concerts chill. Louisa would accompany him after each performance as he left the venue, holding his arm like they were a couple. It worked like a charm, and the fans seemed to be respectful of Louisa's presence by his side all the way to a waiting town car. As they talked while being chauffeured, Michael got to know Louisa, and over time he began to know her as a person as if they had been on real dates.

Over the next several months their relationship began to develop into a friendship and began to engender other feelings. Michael not only enjoyed being with Louisa, who had a great sense of humor, but both also loved music. He was impressed that she always had an empathetic way about her that made his fans even love her. He decided to ask her out on a real date between the concerts. Louisa was surprised and thrilled by the invitation, as she had had the biggest crush on Michael for a long time. They quickly found as they talked over dinner that they had similar interests in so many common areas: family, music, sports and doing charitable work. Within a month they had moved past the holding-hands stage.

After a grueling schedule performing on stage and doing promotional meet and greet sessions in Orlando, Florida, they had a room service dinner in his hotel suite. Michael was totally exhausted and went to the couch and leaned back and closed his eyes for a moment then opened them to see Louisa looking concerned.

"Come and sit with me. I'm a basket case tonight and not very good company."

Louisa sat next to him and put his head on her shoulder and rubbed his temples gently. "Michael, you need a vacation and time to recharge. You'll have a week off before going to Atlanta. Why don't I find you a place in the Keys where it's quiet and the beach is sandy, and the water is warm. What do you say?"

Michael sat up, energized just thinking about Louisa's offer. "You know, that is a terrific idea. Let's do it and I'll tell Gerry later. Of course, you would have to come...but only if you want to."

"If I could sing the yes, I would. Of course, I want to be with you."

When they arrived at the secluded three-bedroom villa, the sun was hot so they didn't waste any time and went for a glorious swim. Exhausted by their exercise and playful splashing, they walked very slowly out of the water and collapsed under an umbrella on a blanket. Both closed their eyes and fell asleep in minutes. Louisa was awakened by the quickening of the breeze as dusk settled in. Michael was still sleeping soundly so she waited another half-hour, watching him with affection before waking him up by gently rubbing his arm until he opened his eyes.

"Okay, sleepyhead, it's been a long day in the Florida sunshine. We both need something to eat and then a good night's sleep."

Michael looked at Louisa appraisingly. His eyes reflected his amorous feelings. "I think I also need a hot shower to refresh and get the sand off, how about you?"

"Never thought you would ask."

Michael and Louisa had a quick bite to eat and had their shower, but they didn't get much sleep that night as they found comfort in each other's arms and other places. They did relax on the beach and swam in the clear water every day. Their time together not only renewed Michael's energy, but it also solidified their feelings about each other. When they arrived in Atlanta for the next concert, their smiling and tanned faces were a giveaway as to where the two had disappeared.

Michael loved to explore the cities where they performed. Louisa would be there to give out memorabilia to his fans or run interference if necessary. After winning a Grammy award, his career was going so well he had to have a security guy follow him, even on dates with Louisa. When they performed in Rome, Michael asked Louisa to drive up to visit Aurelio on their day off.

Aurelio immediately connected with Louisa as she spoke to him in an Italian dialect that she learned from her grandparents. The three of them spent the day touring the vineyard and winery and then went into Siena for dinner at Osteria Permalico. When they entered, several diners recognized Michael and asked for his autograph, which he signed on their cloth napkins. One exuberant woman kept hugging him until Louisa went over and took the woman's arm firmly.

"La smetta per favore, è il mio fidanzato." (Please stop... that's my fiancé.)

The woman stepped back and nodded and walked away quickly, as other patrons began to clap for Louisa who was embarrassed and returned to her seat. Michael and his grandfather exchanged looks of appreciation for Louisa's initiative. After they returned to the farmhouse, Aurelio took Michael aside.

"Michael, I like your new friend, she's a very nice person."

"Very talented too. She's a violinist. Sometimes she'll do a solo at my concerts."

"Next time have her come with her violin. I'd love to hear her play."

"I'm sure she'd love to. How are things going around here?"

"The last grape crop wasn't so great. It cut into our volume, but this season's looking very good."

"If you ever need anything, you know I have money."

"I'm good, and thanks for the offer...I just hope the Mariano winery is doing better. Last time I talked to Francesco, he was concerned."

"Tell them if they need any financial assist to tide them over, I'd be happy to help. That reminds me, I never followed up to contact Sophia since I was here last."

"You should call. Sophia visited me and was sorry she missed your call last time. Sophia has been very thoughtful, bringing me things when she goes shopping."

"I'll do it right now. Maybe we could all get together, and she could meet Louisa?"

Aurelio gave a look of concern while Michael went to the phone to call Sophia. Maria answered.

"Hi, Mrs. Mariano, it's Michael. I'm here visiting my grandfather again...I wonder if I could speak to Sophia."

Michael sensed Maria was guarded in the way she responded. "Oh, yes, Michael...ah...Sophia is away on a trip...she won't be back for another three weeks."

"Is she all right?"

"Oh yes...she is doing fine. I will tell her you called... How is my friend Manuela?"

"Good. My mom is well and at home working."

"Give her my regards when you see her."

Maria hung up before Michael could reply. He stood holding the phone, wondering why Sophia would be traveling for several weeks. Louisa came into the room and saw Michael looking confused.

"Anything happen?"

"No. I was talking to my grandfather's neighbor... It's been a long time since we talked. I guess everyone moves on."

"Isn't change what life is all about? It's one of those constants. It would probably be boring if things always stayed the same."

"What makes you so wise? We must get back to Rome for tomorrow's show. We'll have to leave soon. I'm going to talk to my grandfather for a few minutes and say goodbye then we should go."

"I'm ready anytime."

After their emotional goodbyes, Michael and Louisa began the drive back to Rome.

"I was really happy you and my grandfather got along so well. He's always been a special influence since I was a kid. I was thinking, since we hang with each other so much on the tour, why don't you move in with me when we get back to the states? I bought this nice old house in Greenwich that sees my caretaker more than me. It could use a woman's touch."

Louisa looked over at Michael with her eyes full of love.

"I'd love to. First I have to tell you something that might change your mind."

"What? Please don't tell me you found a new lover in the vineyard."

"No. I want you to be serious. When I was a teenager, I had Hodgkin lymphoma. It's...it's a type of cancer. My parents brought me to the best hematology and oncology doctors they could find. They were able to treat me successfully with chemotherapy. After the six-month treatment protocol, I was told I was in full remission. But the doctor said there was always the possibility of it recurring."

"I'm so sorry. That must have been a terrible thing to go through as a teen. I think we should get you a second opinion by the best specialist we can find in New York City so you don't have to worry."

"I just want to be open about this. I care about us."

"That's why we should move in together when we get back."

"I love you Michael. Being with you has been the happiest time in my life. I just don't want you to ever regret it."

Michael reached over to caress her face. "I don't want you to ever talk about regrets, okay?"

Louisa put her hand gently over his. "Okay!"

After they returned home, they consulted with a top hematologist who ordered tests and then confirmed her understanding.

"Louisa does not show any indication signs of a relapse. Statistically once this disease is in remission there's an 85% chance it won't reoccur, but Louisa is correct. There are no total guarantees."

As they drove back from the doctor's office, Louisa became thoughtful.

"Michael, I want you to be sure you are still okay with my moving in with you."

"Nothing you or the doctor said that changes how I feel about you. I'm all in if you are."

Louisa leaned over and kissed his cheek. "Are you kidding? I fell in love the first time I was in the orchestra, and you sang that gushy old love song, 'Help Me Make It Through the Night,' which was probably written a hundred years ago."

"Not quite. 1970 would be more precise; Kris Kristofferson wrote it...and it's not that gushy, is it?"

Louisa hit him on the shoulder playfully. "Smartass! You're a walking encyclopedia about these old songs. By the way, to me gushy is a good thing."

Michael smiled. "Then gushy you get!"

Michael started singing "Help Me Make It Through the

Night" acapella as he drove.

Louisa sat back and closed her eyes and smiled with happy tears at the corner of her eyes, then put her hand on his shoulder and squeezed it gently.

Michael told Louisa he had meetings in the city and she should move her things to the home he had purchased two years ago in Greenwich, Connecticut. When she arrived, Michael's caretaker, Antonio, was there to show her through the fifty-two-hundred-square-foot renovated Colonial that had been built in 1856. Louisa was overwhelmed by the house's size and grandeur compared to her six-hundred-foot apartment in Greenwich Village. After the house tour, Antonio suggested that Louisa take a walk around the nineteen acres. Immediately she felt she was in heaven as she strolled through the beautiful gardens that were magnificently kept. When she sat on the spacious veranda, she was overwhelmed looking over the sheer beauty of the place—the well-groomed lawn, the white fence enclosed fifty-foot swimming pool. Behind the pool was a regulation size basketball court and, in the distance, a fenced in tennis court.

Just then Antonio came out to see how Louisa was doing.

"Antonio, did Michael add the pool and other facilities?"

Antonio laughed. "The only thing Michael added was that basketball setup."

Michael and Louisa began living together and became a devoted couple. Michael not only found Louisa to be physically attractive, but he also loved her kind heart and gentle ways with people and that their family values were in sync. He asked Louisa to set up a time to meet her family and he brought Louisa to meet Manuela and their new pet DeeDee. Manuela and Louisa hit it off right away and DeeDee found a new loving person to give her lots of pets and treats. As Louisa hugged the willing pet, Manuela watched Michael smile as he lovingly watched Louisa and DeeDee.

As Michael and Louisa left with DeeDee on a leash, Manuela had come outside to wave goodbye. As they reached the car and were putting the pet in the backseat, Louisa put her hand on Michael's back.

"Michael, I think your mom's shared custody arrangement is brilliant since you love this furball and you travel so much."

Michael nodded, kissed Louisa on the cheek and gave Manuela a thumb's up before driving away.

Louisa called her parents, who lived in the Shore Road area in Brooklyn, to tell them her new boyfriend Michael wanted to meet them. Lillian Romano was thrilled that her daughter found someone who wanted to meet her family.

"Why don't you come on Sunday? Then your brother and sister could also meet your young man."

Louisa checked with Michael, who nodded his agreement.

"Michael said he'd love to meet the whole family. We'll be there around one o'clock. "

On Sunday, the family was anxiously waiting to meet Louisa's new beau. Her sister Margaret and brother Rocco were looking out the front window when a chauffeured town car drove up. Louisa hadn't mentioned Michael's last name on the phone so when her sibling's saw Michael Ventura get out of the car and escort Louisa toward the front stairs, Rocco was shocked, and Margaret started to scream but controlled herself. Margaret quickly told her parents the name of Louisa's famous boyfriend. Mrs. Romano said she remembered that Louisa had sent her a CD of his songs because she was in the orchestra.

By the time Michael and Louisa entered, the family had composed themselves and welcomed the couple with hugs and cheek kisses. When Margaret hugged Michael a little too long and too tight, Louisa gave her a raised eyebrow message to cool it. Mr. Romano, who was clueless about his daughter's boyfriend's celebrity, greeted Michael normally and asked if he would like some wine. Michael said he would and talked about his grandfather Aurelio's winery. Michael had conversations with each of the family members and told them how their talented Louisa was as a brilliant violinist and how much help she was to him. Her parents and siblings were delighted hearing Michael's effusive compliments about their Louisa's talents. Embarrassed by Michael's over the top praises, Louisa whispered to Michael to please cool that flattering stuff. He smiled then continued to make her blush and her parents beam, hearing about their amazing child from a famous entertainer.

As they all began to sit down to have dinner, the doorbell rang. Margaret got up to answer it. When she saw it was their neighbor Mrs. Costa who lived across the street, she rolled her eyes and opened the door a crack.

"Hi, Mrs. Costa, we were just sitting down to have lunch."

Mrs. Costa pushed the door open and entered the vestibule, almost knocking Margaret over.

"So lovely to see you here Margaret. I saw your sister and her friend getting out of that car. I baked a cake to welcome her home and would love to see her, and of course meet her new friend."

Hearing the commotion, Louisa got up to see what happened to her sister, and was stopped in her tracks as Mrs. Costa rushed past Margaret and pushed the cake into her hands.

"Louisa! There you are, it's so nice to see you after all this time. I baked this for you and your friend and would love to meet him."

"We were just sitting..."

That didn't stop the aggressive neighbor, who tried to get past her just as Michael came to see what the ruckus was all about. Mrs. Costa practically lifted him off his feet hugging him.

"I am your biggest fan! I have two of your albums! When I saw you get out of the car, I couldn't believe that you would be here in our little neighborhood visiting my best friends."

Michael had to catch his breath after Mrs. Costa's bear hug. As he engaged her in small talk, he turned her around and escorted her to the front door.

"I really appreciate that you like my music, but the Romano's just served the dinner and it would be rude for me not to eat with them. I'm sure as their best friend you understand."

Michael signaled Margaret to open the door.

"It's been so nice meeting you...I will send the family an extra ticket for you when I perform at Madison Square Garden."

Michael walked onto the front stoop with Mrs. Costa and before he could close the door, Mrs. Costa put up her hand for him not to close it.

"Could you also leave a ticket for my daughter, Rosalie?"

Michael controlled his reaction to her chutzpa and just gave a friendly wave. "Of course, I will, Mrs. Costa."

As Michael quietly closed the door, Margaret looked at him with admiration

"That was rad the way you handled her. I thought we'd end up with her using the guest room bed, with you tied to it."

Michael laughed. "I don't think she would have been that bad. Some encounters I have been are hairy...just ask your sister, but not until after we eat."

Louisa came over, still holding the cake from Mrs. Costa. "At least you inspired her to bring dessert."

Michael put his arms around the two sisters and led them back to the dining room. Louisa couldn't help but smile as Michael charmed her family with his casual conversation and self-deprecating humor.

After dinner, he played the piano and sang for them an old Dean Martin hit, "That's Amore." She glowed, watching her family enjoying themselves.

When the family visit was over, Louisa went to check if their ride was there. As she opened the door to leave, the town car was indeed waiting to take them home, along with a crowd of neighbors waiting on the sidewalk in front of the Romano house.

"Michael, there's good news and not so good news. The car is here but you have some neighbors waiting to meet you. Mrs. Costa must've shared with everyone in the neighborhood."

"No problem, let's go and meet the neighbors."

Michael said his goodbyes to the Romano's, hugging each one, and then went out to greet the neighbors. He was charming and accessible, signing autographs for some and getting and giving hugs all around.

As Michael and Louisa were being driven home, Louisa put her hand on his arm.

"My parents adored you. My sister has a big crush, and my brother wants to take you fishing. They all were amazed that you were so normal because they thought celebrities were different beings. Then you were so nice to the neighbors. My mom was standing at the top of the stairs so proud."

"You have a great family. I think we should help your folks, so they don't have to worry in their old age. Find out if they have a mortgage and we'll pay it off. Let's set up a bank account for you where they are also signatories. This way they always have access if they need something."

"Michael, you are too much. That you thought of helping my family after you just met them."

"La tua famiglia è la mia famiglia." (Your family is my family.)

Louisa squeezed his arm, put her head on his shoulder, and smiled. "And your Italian is not so bad either."

Michael and Louisa were married the next year, with the help of Gerry Needham, at a small chapel in the Guardian

Angel Cathedral while on tour in Las Vegas. The ceremony was without fanfare or publicity. Billy, his friend, and one of Louisa's orchestra buddies served as witnesses. Their low-key nuptials not only disappointed their relatives and friends, but the publicist was also off the wall hearing about it a week later. Gerry had pizza brought to their reception in their hotel suite. Gerry, Billy and one of Louisa's musician friends toasted them with bottles of wine from Aurelio's private collection. Aurelio called Michael and said he was happy for him. He thought Louisa was a great choice. When Michael called Manuela, she was happy he had married in a church but a little put out by not being invited. She said when they were back in town, they must have a reception for family and friends. Michael agreed and said he would host it at his house in Greenwich when they were back from the tour next month.

The next time they were back in the New York area, Michael was true to his word and catered a reception for his relatives, Louisa's family and their friends who were able to come. Gerry arranged for several top talents to come and entertain. Michael was so moved by their showing up, he joined in by singing a Frank Sinatra hit, "Fly Me to The Moon." As he started to sing, he took Louisa by the hand and sang it to her.

At the end of the song, he kissed Louisa tenderly and was toasted by everyone who was moved by his expression of love. There were tears in her mom's eyes at the end of the song and her sister Margaret was so overcome, she ran over and hugged them both. The celebration went so long, many of the guests had to stay over.

Michael and Louisa agreed they both wanted to lead a quiet life when not touring. They spent as much time at their house as they could. Louisa enjoyed working in the garden, learning about the different flowers and plants from the gardener. Michael loved shooting hoops by himself and playing Horse with friends and neighbors. Unfortunately, their efforts to have a child over the years were not successful. They enjoyed good times at home, sometimes having friends, family and colleagues over. They also enjoyed occasionally going out to dinner with friends and finding interesting places while on tour. Michael's career was at a peak with record sales in the millions and sold-out concerts in every city. Whatever else was happening around them, they kept trying to have a child. It was a big disappointment to the couple when it didn't happen.

Chapter 10

LIFE THROWS A CURVE

Michael and Louisa decided to seek the advice of a fertility specialist. After a series of blood tests and other prescribed protocols, Louisa was told that her hyperthyroidism condition might be the cause and would account for her symptoms, including her inability to gain weight even though she ate heartily. She immediately began his prescribed treatment for the condition. Michael also had his sperm checked to see if he could be the reason they couldn't conceive. When his tests came back, they found there was no issue from his side. When her treatments ended, Louisa was still unable to conceive. Michael suggested they consult with Dr. Warren Kelly, a top hematology/oncology specialist, who ordered a series of tests and exams for Louisa to get to the bottom of the problem. Over a period of several weeks, Louisa was subjected to blood tests, sonograms, pelvic and laparoscopic exams. Dr. Kelly called Michael and said he had reviewed everything and asked that they both come in.

After he sat them down, Dr. Kelly told them that Louisa's

earlier chemotherapy treatments might also have been the secondary reason for not conceiving but there was a more serious thing to discuss. The biopsy they took revealed that the lymphoma had recurred. He recommended and they agreed to aggressively treat it over a period of many months. Michael had all his concerts canceled so he could be with Louisa through the ordeal. He stayed by her side when she became weak and overwhelmed by the spreading cancer. He had a cot brought to her hospital room and stayed during the night. Michael woke up frequently to see if she needed anything. Her family and Manuela also came frequently to see her and tried to bolster her spirits and comfort Michael. Louisa was declining faster than even her doctors thought. Michael was at her side with her family for the visit by Father Donatuer, the family's pastor from St. Patrick's Church on 95th Street in Brooklyn. He asked them to leave and then administered the "anointing of the sick rites" and said prayers with Louisa, who passed peaceably within hours of his visit.

Michael was not only bereft, but he also felt guilty that they didn't discover it sooner and he couldn't save her despite all his fame and money. As he went through Louisa's personal things, he found the savings account statement of the joint account he funded for her and her parents. It still was untouched at the initial million dollars and had some accrued interest. Neither Louisa nor her folks had withdrawn any of the money. It reminded him that he wasn't the only one who lost Louisa.

Michael decided to arrange for a one-night wake at a funeral home in Brooklyn, near the Romano home. Manuela came with him and was a comfort to the grieving family. The neighborhood also turned out in droves that day to support the family and then surrounded him with affection when he arrived for the seven o'clock viewing.

The priest came over to Michael and told him that he

believed Louisa would already be watching them from heaven. Michael teared up and thanked him for making Louisa's last day more peaceful. Before he left at the end of the night, Michael asked Margaret to meet him in the office of the funeral director, where he handed her the bank statement and asked to help her parents access the funds when they had recovered from their loss. He added that if the family ever needed him, he would always be there for them. He gave her a hug and said he had to leave but would see them at the church for the requiem mass in the morning. He requested the funeral director make arrangements to pick up the family in the morning to take them to the church, then to the cemetery and back home so they wouldn't have to worry about transportation. Margaret thanked him for his generosity and thoughtfulness, but most of all for loving and caring for her sister.

After the burial, Gerry called several times to tell him he needed to see him. Michael kept begging off, thinking Gerry wanted him to go on tour. There was no way he was ready to go on a stage and sing love songs after he lost Louisa. Gerry finally came to his home and handed him a sealed letter.

"I'm sorry, but Louisa asked me to give this to you if she didn't make it." Gerry became very emotional and teared up and said he had to leave.

"Your Louisa was a dear, dear person. We all miss her."

Michael nodded and took the letter inside and opened it.

"Dearest Michael, when you get this note, I will have passed, hopefully to a place I can still see you flourish as a wonderful, loving man and great talent to share with the world.

I want you not to be too sad that I'm gone because, in our short time together, you made me the happiest woman that was blessed to be with someone so generous with his love for me and helpful to those less fortunate. When you are ready, I want you to find someone special who you will love and that she will give you back all the love and support you deserve.

Love Always, Louisa."

Michael put up his hands in frustration and called out loud.

"Oh God, why did she have to leave me? Please take good care of her, she is very special."

Michael was crying as he stared at the letter, then read it again. He wiped the tears from his eyes and then folded the letter carefully, put it back in its envelope. He kissed it and placed it in the center of the table and cried again.

Michael in his grief became a social isolate, avoiding everyone important to him including Manuela, Gerry and Billy. His pet DeeDee became his only regular companion. She would climb up on the couch and put her head on his lap and not move until he petted her head. When he went to bed, DeeDee would lay on the floor next to him. When Aurelio called him after Manuela sought the grandfather's help to bring Michael out of his depression, his mood did perk while they talked. Michael promised while they talked to visit his grandfather. Instead, he began watching movies on several streaming services. Watching videos on YouTube of some of the old crooners reminded him of his visits to Italy. When he listened to the sweet but sad song "Honey," about a wife who died, it reminded him again of his own loss. Manuela arrived with Gerry in hopes of shaking him out of his funk. While he enjoyed their visit, when they left, his mood became dark again.

Chapter 11

FAMILY MATTERS

Manuela urgently called Michael a month later to give him more distressing news.

"Your grandfather had a blocked artery and required emergency surgery. He is in intensive care at University Hospital in Siena. Pietro said it happened while he was chopping firewood for that wood-burning stove he has in his office. He had to be rushed to the emergency room and then have a stent surgically inserted to get the blood flowing. He's in recovery and the doctors say he should be okay, but I'm very worried. Would you please come with me?"

Manuela's call shocked Michael out of his depression.

"I'll make the reservations immediately to leave tonight. You start packing. I'll call you with the time and I'll drop off DeeDee at that boarding place she loves on the way."

Michael quickly made the arrangements by calling Gerry, who had the best travel agent. He was elated to hear from Michael. When he was told what happened, Gerry quickly made all the arrangements himself for the flight that night to

Rome. He also arranged for a car rental then called Michael with the information. Michael called the pet boarding service then went to his bedroom, took his suitcase and quickly packed. On his way out, he went back to the living room and put Louisa's letter carefully into a jacket pocket. He called their airport car service and then texted Manuela with the time he would pick her up. He put the leash on DeeDee and told the pet she was going to have play dates for a few weeks. He brought the suitcase out onto the porch and walked DeeDee around the property until the car service arrived.

When their plane landed in Rome later than planned because of a weather delay, Michael caused a stir as they disembarked at Fiumicino International Airport. He was recognized by an Italian fan who pointed him out to the crowd. Michael and Manuela had to escape the growing crowds of people by signing autographs as he moved quickly to the car rental counter. They quickly processed the rental papers and escorted him out the back of the building to a beautiful 700-series cashmere silver BMW. As they handed Michael the remote starter, his face reflected that he was pleasantly surprised and impressed with Gerry's choice. He turned to see his mom was also more than a little wide-eyed.

"Gerry outdid himself. I better thank him and let him know we arrived safely."

Michael sat in the driver's seat and took his international cellphone and texted Gerry.

"Arrived safely, thank you. The car is beautiful, it's too much. I love it."

The traffic getting out of Rome was a problem, but once clear of the congestion, they quickly drove to the hospital in Siena in two-and-a-half hours. Just as they were pulling into the parking lot, the Mariano family was exiting. They had hoped to see Michael after so many years, but left just minutes before his arrival because Sophia had learned through her smart phone that their flight had been delayed.

When Michael and Manuela entered the hospital, they were stopped on the way to the room by two excited nurses who recognized him. Michael graciously stopped for a minute to talk to them. One of the nurses said she had cared for Aurelio when he was first admitted and was in recovery from the surgery.

"Tuo padre è un gentiluomo meraviglioso lo adorano tutti."

Michael looked at Manuela to translate.

"The nurse said your grandfather is a wonderful gentleman and everyone loves him."

Michael took the nurses hand and shook it. "Grazie...thank you so much for caring for him."

The nurse shrugged, not understanding. Manuela smiled at the nurse.

"Grazie per come ti prendi cura di lui."

The nurse smiled and quickly kissed Michael on both cheeks then left quickly. The other nurse did the same then hurried away.

Manuela was amused. "You sure have an effect on the ladies."

Michael put up his hands, not knowing what to say to that. "I'm surprised anyone remembers me. Come, let's just go and see your dad."

Aurelio was still weak from the surgery but happy to see his daughter and famous grandson. Within minutes of their arrival, a transport team entered and announced they were taking Aurelio for a blood transfusion. The attending nurse asked them to leave so he could rest that night and let the transfusion work overnight so he could regain his strength. Michael and Manuela agreed that was a good idea and they would come back the next day. As they left, a group of nurses were in the hall waiting for Michael. Each gave him a two-cheek Italian greeting while Manuela watched in amusement. They left quickly after Michael thanked each of the nurses for their service. When he turned toward her, Manuela saw the lipstick marks. She reached into her pocketbook and handed him a tissue.

"Nobody remembers you... Right."

Michael just shrugged as Manuela reached out to hold both his arms and moved in close.

"I think everyone misses you."

Manuela drove the car while Michael leaned on the headrest, resting. When they exited the car in front of the Ventura farmhouse, Michael stopped to look around and breathed in the fresh country air deeply and smiled.

"I really shouldn't have been away so long."

Pietro came out to welcome them and kissed Manuela on both cheeks then hugged Michael tightly.

"Michael, I want to tell you how sorry I am for your loss of that dear sweet woman."

"I wanted to thank you for your Mass card and your beautiful letter. Her family and I were also grateful for the beautiful flowers you sent to the funeral home."

"It's important that you came to be with Aurelio. I know he felt bad not being able to travel to be with there for you, but he already was not feeling well. I think the sadness about Louisa's passing and the stress of not going to be with you made him feel worse. Chopping wood for his precious woodburning stove put the final pressure on the artery. My good friend didn't know he was in such bad shape until he felt the pressure on his chest that morning. When the crew arrived with the ambulance, they had to use a defibrillator to revive him before they transported him to the hospital. The emergency room doctor saved his life by getting him immediately to the surgeon who inserted the stent. Apparently normal tests don't necessarily show blockage. From what I researched; an echocardiogram should be a required procedure for older patients to find blockages to help prevent this from happening."

Michael listened intently to the winery manager about his grandfather's close call.

"Mom and I are so grateful that you were here to call the ambulance and that everyone did their best to save him. It's a tribute to your medical system."

When they entered the farmhouse, Michael dropped the suitcases and went immediately into Aurelio's office, where he had listened to the record collection with him so long ago. He took out a few of the records to look at and smiled remembering playing them, which brought back fond memories of being with his grandfather. As he walked around, Michael spotted a picture on a side cabinet. It was a photo of him when he was fourteen with his friend Sophia mugging for the camera. While it brought back fond memories, it also made him realize that a long time had passed since he was in contact with Sophia. He remembered her kind letter of condolence and the Mass card she sent after his dad died, then the flowers and Mass card for Louisa. Michael turned on the record player and listened to an old song they shared. He started to smile thinking about the two of them playing in the fields, kicking the soccer ball and swimming in their underwear as kids in the nearby lake. Those were good times and Sophia was a special friend until his life went in a totally different direction. Then he remembered that their last time together was at the window watching the Palio and it made him laugh about his embarrassing immature reaction.

Michael sat on the couch and leaned back his head on the pillow, holding the framed photo. The hectic quick trip and jet lag finally caught up and he quickly fell asleep. Manuela came to the office to see how Michael was doing and became curious about what he was holding. She tiptoed in and shut down the record player, removed the photo from his hand and smiled when she saw who was in it. Manuela found a throw cover in the closet, put it over him and quietly shut the door.

The next morning, Michael and Manuela were up early. After breakfast, they stopped by to visit the Ventura Winery to talk with Pietro, who told them not to worry about day-to-day operations. He would take care of the winery, but Aurelio usually took care of the business side so they should ask him about that if he was well enough. Michael reached out for Pietro's hand and they shook on it.

On the way back to Siena the next morning, Manuela said she would like to attend Siena Cathedral's morning Mass and say a prayer for Aurelio's recovery before heading to visit him. Michael shrugged his okay and entered the new destination in the car's GPS system.

As they began to enter the church, Michael waved off an approaching fan indicating he had to get into the church on time. As he moved into the pew, he looked around and returned knowing smiles from parishioners but didn't recognize that the person two pews in front of him was his childhood friend Sophia, now a fully grown beautiful woman. Toward the end of Mass, when the congregation exchanged the "peace be with you" exchange (La pace sia con te), Michael and Sophia nodded to each other. She smiled broadly, finally seeing her childhood friend in person. When Michael gave her a curious look, trying to remember if he knew her, Sophia was disappointed and hurt. She forgot for the moment that she recognized him in maturity because he was an international celebrity who she followed on various media. Now a well-endowed grown woman, Sophia was no longer the gangly young teenager he once knew.

At the end of the service, Sophia deliberately waited until Michael and Manuela left the church then followed discretely at a distance. Sophia watched Michael being recognized by a female fan who rushed over to greet him. Churchgoers started to surround him. The reality that Michael was so well known confirmed for Sophia that he probably forgot her completely. Michael and Manuela walked quickly while acknowledging the attention of the crowd signing the occasional autograph when someone thrust it at him. After they got into the car, Michael turned to Manuela.

"Did you happen to notice the woman two pews in front of me during the peace greeting? She gave me a big smile and nodded like we knew each other, and there was something familiar about her."

Manuela shook her head no. "I was talking to the woman behind me. She thought she recognized you and asked me if I knew who you were."

"What did you tell her?"

"That you were my son."

Michael laughed, gave Manuela a loving hand squeeze. "This son thinks his mom is pretty cool."

Michael then started the car and drove off quickly.

Aurelio was sitting up in bed when Manuela and Michael came in. The blood transfusion had made a big difference in his energy and physical appearance. He reached up and hugged them both and thanked them for making the long trip. He asked about their flight and the drive from Rome. Manuela took his hand.

"Everything was great...now tell me; what did the doctors say about what you need to do to recuperate?"

"I have to take some meds for at least a year, one of them is a blood thinner, and I must follow a particular dietary program listed on this sheet and walk for exercise. They said no chopping wood. They're sending a special nurse to go over everything tomorrow."

"That's good. We'll come and listen with you."

"That would be helpful. Did you get to see the Mariano

family when you came here yesterday? Sophia left with her parents just before you arrived, she somehow saw on her phone that your flight was delayed."

Michael nodded. "It was and we didn't see them. They were probably in a different parking area. Coincidently, I did go into your office last night and found a picture on a cabinet with my old friend Sophia. I even played one of your old records and remembered how she loved listening to your collection when we'd sneak into your office without you knowing."

Aurelio grinned. "Sorry, Michael. I did know about your visits, and I was happy that you and Sophia enjoyed one of my favorite past times. That reminds me, please thank the Mariano family for bringing me these beautiful flowers. I wonder if you wouldn't mind checking with Pietro and making sure he had what he needed to keep the business side of the operation going? You'll find all the office keys and the combination to my safe in the back of the right drawer of my desk. I'm so grateful you came to help me. I know losing Louisa has been a terrible blow. I'm sure dealing with it has been very difficult. When I lost your grandmother, I was so depressed, it took a long time for me to deal with it. Try to find a way to heal while you're here. I can tell you from experience that happiness is being with the people you care about. I know because your being here has made me very happy."

Manuela bent over and kissed her dad. "You get some rest. Don't worry about the business. We'll take care of everything until you are home and able to take charge."

Michael gave Aurelio a loving kiss on the cheek. "They will keep you a day or two more to be sure you're okay. Please do what they tell you and we'll come tomorrow to listen to what they recommend as a follow-up. Call if we can bring anything."

As Michael and Manuela walked to his car, a group of well-dressed women visitors were getting out of a new Mercedes next to Michael's car. One of the women recognized him and yelled loudly.

"Sei Michael Ventura...amo le tue canzoni." (You're Michael Ventura...I love your songs.)

Michael waved. "Grazie l'ho apprezzato." (Thank you, I appreciate it).

He quickly got in the car. Manuela was looking ahead with a straight face and hadn't put on her seatbelt.

"How about that. One day in Italy and my son speaks the language."

Michael looked over and grinned, then hit the gas hard and made Manuela fall back against the seat.

When she readjusted herself, Manuela smiled to herself and hit Michael's arm with a light tap.

"I'm your mother, so be careful."

"I'm the driver, so put on your seatbelt."

At the farmhouse, Michael and Manuela found the keys in the desk where Aurelio had instructed. They took the time to look through the material in Aurelio's office. Much of it was somewhat confusing to Michael because headings were written in Italian. Manuela translated as they compiled a list of things to do.

The next day Michael visited the Mariano farmhouse to thank them for visiting Aurelio. Marie and Francesco were happy to see him and congratulated him on his success. As they shared a coffee, Maria told him that Sophia was teaching at the Scuola Superiore (high school). "Sophia has been following your career and is proud of your success. Sophia was very saddened by your father's death and then the loss of your wife."

Michael choked a bit. "What subject does Sophia teach?"

"I thought you knew. She is the language teacher. She teaches Italian and English classes. After you had to return home so quickly that summer, she was going to surprise you by speaking English better. Even when you didn't come back, she continued to study English through high school and then at the University."

Michael felt a tinge of regret for not knowing she was serious about learning his language. "I had no idea she was doing that! Please tell Sophia I will stop by again and that I'd really like to see her and apologize for not staying in touch. "

Just as he was leaving, a young boy was walking toward the house. Michael was curious.

"Hi, I'm Michael. What's your name?"

The boy stepped back from him. "Sono Michele, abito qui." (I'm Michele, I live here.)

Before Michael could ask another question, the child ran quickly by him and into the Mariano farmhouse. Michael stopped to look back and overheard him say to Maria.

"Nonna c'era un uomo qui fuori che ho visto in TV una volta...mi ha chiesto il mio nome."

"I know... He's an old friend...he has the same name as you in English...his name in English is Michael."

Michael walked to his rental car, puzzled by the boy's presence at the Mariano's.

The next morning, Michael met with Pietro about what was needed to keep the vineyard's business on track while Aurelio recuperated. Before they left for Siena, Michael and Manuela discussed their plans to help with the business. Both decided to extend their stay and help Aurelio until he was back on his feet. After settling their commitment to help Aurelio during his recovery and stay longer, Manuela started to leave the room. Michael stopped her by holding her by the arm.

"Mom, one more thing. Yesterday, I met this boy at the Mariano farmhouse. He said his name was Michele. Do you know anything about him?"

Manuela looked surprised.

"Of course, Michele, he's about nine years or ten years old by now. He's Sophia's son from her marriage to Lorenzo. I thought you knew."

Michael shrugged, indicating he didn't know. "I guess I've been clueless and thoughtless about a lot of things. Please tell me."

Manuela sat down and gestured him to sit.

"Sophia had a short marriage to a man named Lorenzo. Maria told me they met at the University of Rome. The man was a real charmer; smart, handsome and rich but unfortunately not very loyal. His dad is a major wine exporter. I think they were divorced shortly after Michele was born. He told Sophia he didn't want to be tied down. Your old friend found out later he was having multiple affairs. It was very upsetting for Sophia because she is religious. I think she was even able to get an annulment on grounds connected with his duplicity. Though they share secular custody, the boy rarely sees his father, who is one of those jetsetters. His grandfather left him a fortune and from what Maria said, he is spending it as fast as he can. Unfortunately for Sophia, there is only a small amount he pays in child support because Sophia refused to challenge the divorce settlement. I think she just wanted to be out of a bad marriage."

Michael put up his hands in a gesture of his frustration. "I had no idea that Sophia had to deal with all that. I really do have to see her. She was a dear friend when we were young and I got so caught up in my own stuff when Dad died, then my career and losing Louisa, I ignored her when she wrote to me and then completely forgot my friend."

Manuela put her hand gently on Michael's arm. "So now you have a chance to help your grandfather and fix it with Sophia."

Michael nodded. "You're right. I'm here to help and Sophia only lives on the other side of the gate."

The next two days were very challenging for Michael as he worked hard in the vineyard helping the pickers. He became energized by the physical work and the men and began singing with them. When the day was over, he went back to the farmhouse. He tried reading the mail and checking the ledger but had to ask his mom to translate. He remembered Aurelio's words reminding him to take some time to relax and reconnect with those he cared about. Michael saw the photo again of him and Sophia before their trip to Siena. It reminded him that last time they were together was at the window at the Palio. Manuela heard the frame click and looked up at Michael. He appeared to be distressed about something as he was turning to leave.

"Michael, what's going on?"

He turned back to look at his mother and at that moment, he made a decision.

Chapter 12

FINDING SOPHIA

Michael rushed past Manuela to take a shower and came back neat and clean.

"I'm going now to drop by the Mariano Vineyard and see Sophia."

Manuela's look of concern turned to a smile. "Give her my best."

As Michael arrived, he saw Michele playing by himself kicking a soccer ball. He stopped to kick the ball back to Michele who then returned it, excited there was someone to play with. Michael spent some time kicking and returning the soccer ball. They both sat down to rest, and they discussed the upcoming soccer matches in Michele's spotty English and Michael's limited Italian. Michael was impressed by how informed the boy was about the sport. Maria, who was watching from the window, was happy that Michael was engaging her grandson. That Michele seemed to relate to their neighbor's famous grandson pleased her greatly as she came outside.

"Michael! Sophia called a few minutes ago. She had to stay after to work on some fundraising project for the school. Why don't you just go to the school and surprise her?"

"Grazie...I think I will," Michael said as he turned to Michele.

"I have to go to see your mom, but let's get together next time so you can teach me your moves. I need to learn to kick better"

He moved quickly to his car, entered the school into the GPS and drove away.

Michele waved and ran to Maria.

"Nonna...Quell uomo Michael è un amico di mia madre."

When Michael arrived at the school in the silver BMW, the car caused a stir with several male students who were leaving the school. Michael was just getting out as they rushed over to admire his wheels.

Michael became cautious and stayed by the car.

"Hi guys...can I help you?"

One stepped forward. "Maybe you let us take it for a spin."

Michael good-naturedly wagged his finger at the teen.

"Sorry, my insurance doesn't cover anyone else driving. I have to see one of your teachers, so I have to lock the car, also for insurance reasons."

As Michael headed to the school's entrance, he stopped to look back. The boys were walking around the car still admiring it. When he entered, he was immediately recognized by one of the girl students who yelled out his name excitedly. He was quickly surrounded by a group of teenage girls wondering why a big celebrity was visiting their school. He patiently signed autographs on a notebook for two of the teens. He was impressed they spoke English so well.

"Could one of you show me to Sophia Mariano's classroom?"

One of the girls stepped forward. "I'm Emma. Ms. Mariano

is my teacher. Her class is over, but she will still be in the teachers' lounge. I will take you."

As Michael followed Emma, the other girls followed close behind. When they reached the teachers' lounge, Emma ushered Michael into the room and was followed by all the chattering girls. Sophia had just finished a conversation with one of the teachers and was getting ready to leave. When Emma pointed her out, Michael stopped in his tracks and called out in a loud voice that made everyone in the room stop what they were doing.

"Sophia! That was you at the church."

Michael impulsively rushed past the teachers who were clueless about what was happening. He wrapped his arms around a surprised Sophia and lifted her up with an enthusiastic hug and kissed her on each cheek.

"I can't believe it...it's so good to finally get together. When I saw you at church, I had no idea my little friend had grown to be such a beautiful young woman."

Sophia was overwhelmed by Michael's show of affection and very embarrassed as the teens all cheered. Also, a large crowd of teachers and staff came in from the hall to see what the noise was all about. When one of the women recognized the stranger with their colleague, they clapped spontaneously, surprised their colleague was such a close friend of the famous singer. In the back of the crowd was a frowning science teacher named Matteo and a starry-eyed, attractive female student counselor named Anna.

Flustered by Michael's arrival and all the attention, Sophia said pointedly in a reserved tone of voice.

"It has been a long time, Michael. It's good to see you too. It was nice that you came to help Aurelio. My mother said you came by. I would have come to see you and Manuela, but I didn't want to intrude. I knew how busy you must be. I see some of my students are already fans of yours."

Michael just stood back, still holding Sophia's hands. He looked at her curiously, a little disappointed by her cool reaction but still enthusiastic about finally connecting.

"I know it's been a very long time between visits, and I hope my coming here didn't embarrass you too much. Your mom thought I should come here since I kept missing you at the farmhouse. Maria said you had to stay because you were busy after school with a big project. Incidentally, your students have been terrific and love their teacher. If you are free, I'd really like to take you to dinner and catch up."

Sophia looked over at Matteo, who was visibly annoyed that she was still talking to Michael.

"I can't tonight. I have a previous commitment and need to go home to change. Maybe another time. I'm really sorry you have been through such a difficult time losing your wife."

Michael's whole demeanor suddenly changed, and Sophia was sorry she had brought up Louisa's passing.

"Thank you. It has been very difficult, but my grandfather needed us to be here. I still find it hard to talk about it. Can I at least escort you to your car? I should have realized you had a busy life. Maybe we can get together some other time."

Sophia was touched by Michael's reaction and his sincerity. "Yes! I'd like that. My car is in the teacher's section if you still want to walk with me."

She looked over to Matteo and gestured that she would see him later. He nodded but didn't look happy.

As Michael walked with Sophia to her car, the students followed closely, still chattering about their teacher and her famous visitor. As he opened the driver side door for Sophia, Michael glanced back at the crowd of students who were shouting.

"Torna a trovarci." (Come back to see us.)

When Michael noticed the teacher who Sophia waved to still had a scowl on his face, he waved to him with a friendly gesture then leaned into tease Sophia.

"I think you have an admirer who wants to make me disappear."

Sophia looked over at Matteo, smiled and nodded to him. "That's Matteo. He's a colleague and we've been seeing each other casually for about six months. He teaches science and coaches the wrestling team, so be careful not to make him angry."

Michael smiled at the implied warning, and noticeably lightened up. "I appreciate the heads up and will certainly be careful not to get your boyfriend mad at me."

Sophia reacted to his sudden more upbeat mood change. "I didn't say he was my boyfriend."

Michael teased back. "Don't tell Matteo that. It might make him angry. I'm sorry I showed up unannounced, but I would like to see my old friend when you have time."

"Why don't you come by the house on Saturday for lunch at one o'clock? I know my parents would love to see you."

Michael grasped her hands. "Deal. I will come to see you and your parents on Saturday."

He bent over to kiss Sophia on the cheek just as she turned her head to wave goodbye to the crowd who were still watching from a distance. Their lips touched accidentally, causing both to be flustered and the student onlookers to start clapping again. Michael quickly backed off.

Sophia was taken totally off guard and, not knowing how to react, she drove away quickly. As she drove out of the parking lot, she said out loud to herself. "Oh Michael...what do I do now?"

Michael stood embarrassed as the young students cheered. He gave a hand wave to them and a shoulder shrug to Matteo, trying to indicate the kiss was an accident. Matteo angrily glared as Michael moved quickly to his car. As the students rushed toward him, he waved .

"Ciao, my young friends...I will come back."
Michael slid into the driver's seat and sped off quickly.

Chapter 13

FRIENDSHIP IS COMPLICATED

Michael briefed Manuela and Aurelia about the reception.

"Sophia is involved in a relationship with a fellow teacher who wasn't thrilled by my showing up. I'll tell you one thing; she must be a great teacher because the students love her."

Manuela looked him in the eye. "How did you feel about finally seeing Sophia after all this time?"

Michael thought for a few seconds. "I am very happy that she is doing so well despite her divorce from someone who cheated and didn't take care of his son. I'll see her Saturday when I visit the Mariano family."

Manuela nodded with a knowing smile. "That's good. They are nice people."

Aurelio, who had been listening, put his hands on Michael's shoulder. "Sophia has been a good daughter to her parents and a loving mother to Michele. Her father told me she was raising money to hold a concert to add a lab for the science program and build a new computerized classroom at her school. She feels it's extremely important for the local students to stay up to date on all the technology. Maybe you could help her since you have lots of experience in that area."

Michael put up his hands. "I don't know if that's such a good idea. She has this boyfriend who is also a colleague. I also realized by her reaction today that it's been a very long time since I was her good friend."

Aurelio looked at him and extended his two hands in a loving gesture. "You and Sophia have been living your lives, but you are here now and helping an old friend is a kindness. I have been so proud of you and how you have been so successful and that you turned out to be a good human being. I know you've been through a very difficult time since you lost Louisa. Helping me here and at Sophia's school will help you heal."

Michael squeezed his grandfather's hands. "You were the one who inspired me to be interested in music. I remember how Sophia encouraged me to play those records. We would listen to your collection a lot when we were kids. I'm so happy she became such an amazing teacher and is so popular with the students and her colleagues. I will think about offering to help. Maybe it could make up a little for my absence."

"Come, sing with me like you did when you were a boy."

Aurelio ushered Michael into his office and thought for a minute. He took out one the vinyl records, which was one of his favorite old standards. As it started to play, Aurelio began to sing "All I Do is Dream of You," and signaled Michael to join him.

Manuela, who was standing in the doorway, listened to their duet. When they finished, she started to clap enthusiastically.

"Bravi... Mio padre e mio figlio."

Aurelio and Michael took their bow, and both gave Manuela a group hug.

Michael returned to his room. He smiled when he remembered the accidental kiss and the reaction of Matteo. He put on a jacket and went to see if Pietro still needed help at the winery, because the October harvest was underway. Pietro said they would be kept busy for the rest of the harvest.

Back at the farmhouse, Manuela and Aurelio discussed Michael being in better spirits. They were thrilled that he was singing again. When Manuela came into Michael's room at dusk to ask if he wanted to go with her to visit the Mariano family the next evening, she found him fast asleep. His physically exhausting work in the vineyard was what the doctor ordered. His face had some color and he looked peaceful, which made her smile.

At the Mariano farmhouse the next evening, Manuela shared a cup of coffee with Maria. When Sophia came home, she was happy to see Manuela.

"I'm so happy you came over. Michael dropped by the school yesterday and surprised me. He caused quite a stir with many of our students who now are big fans of his. Did Michael say anything about his visit?"

"Only that he was so excited to see how amazing you were and how proud he was that you were so accomplished and popular at school. He told me what a beautiful woman you are and was impressed that you spoke English like a native and your students were such good English speakers. When I went to talk to him later, he was already asleep on the couch. He's been so tired at the end of the day from all the physical work in the vineyard because of the harvest. That he had the energy to go to the school to see you, it must have been important to him."

Manuela noticed a controlled smile that came over Sophia. "Michael created a great deal of excitement. Today my female students were still having trouble paying attention to their lessons. They only want me to tell them stories about how Michael and I met and what we did together. I'm not quite sure how I'm going to get them focused again."

Maria chimed in. "My Francesco is still out with his field workers. I can imagine how tiring the harvest can be, especially for Michael."

Manuela was surprised by Maria changing the conversation. "Michael actually is used to hard work. When they are on tour, they work long hours. It is wonderful to see him getting outdoors and looking healthy. Sophia, tell me, how is that fundraising concert for the high school doing?"

Sophia shrugged. "It's complicated. The professional entertainment from Rome that we counted on haven't fully committed and some of my committee that were supposed to help didn't do their part."

"That's a shame. I'm sure Michael would be interested in helping you. He has a great deal of experience about these things. Why don't you ask him to be part of your committee?"

"I know how busy Michael must be covering for Aurelio, and I didn't want to put extra pressure on him."

Manuela took Sophia by her shoulders and looked at her with all seriousness. "Getting Michael back to what he loves would be doing him a big favor. Since he lost Louisa, he hasn't been his old self. I think you and this fundraiser concert could be exactly what he needs."

Sophia thought for a moment. "If you think it wouldn't be a burden. To get the famous Michael Ventura on my committee would be tremendous. His name alone would not only assure attendance but probably get some of the talent who are on the fence to want to come. I know the women on the committee would step up just to impress him. If you could ask him off the record, I would come over and bring him up to date on everything."

"Okay, I'll talk to him as soon as I get home, but I'll need a few details to convince him about its worthy goals."

Sophia became excited. "Come to my room and I'll give

you everything you need. In fact, we have a special meeting tomorrow after class for every member to update the committee on their part. If Michael could come, he'd get brought up to date quickly."

The two conspirators left immediately, leaving Maria shaking her head at the turn of events.

When Manuela returned to the Ventura farmhouse, she briefed Michael on the concert issues and made a point that Sophia really needed his help. He hesitated.

"You think I should? It might get awkward."

Manuela came close and looked him straight in the eye.

"When has my son ever been intimidated by anything?"

Chapter 14

HELPING SOPHIA

"If Sophia doesn't think it would be an issue for her, I would love to help such a worthy cause she's involved in. I do owe her that much."

Manuela without hesitation took his arm.

"Sophia was so excited that you might say yes, she invited you to the committee meeting after classes tomorrow so you could catch up. Here's the folder. The time of the meeting is on it."

Michael looked at his mom questioningly. "Wait a minute. Is it you or Sophia who want me to be on this committee?"

"To be honest, both of us."

"Why didn't I know I was being played? I'll study the material and tomorrow I will go to that meeting and if that Matteo guy doesn't like it, that's his problem."

Michael picked up the folder and left the room as Manuela smiled with satisfaction.

The next afternoon Michael came running in from the field all sweaty, unshaven and dirty. Manuela did a double take as he raced by her and Aurelio who were sitting on the porch. Twenty minutes later he came flying out of the farmhouse, clean shaven and dressed up. He waved to them, jumped in the car and raced off. Manuela turned to her dad.

"I think our Michael might be back!"

Aurelio just nodded his agreement with a broad smile.

Michael drove to the school quickly and pulled into the parking lot of the high school just as students were waiting to get into minibuses, while others had their own transportation. As he walked quickly up to the entrance, Emma, his previous student guide, and some of her informal posse rushed to greet him. This caused more students to see what was going on and create a larger crowd to surround him. While flattered by their attention, Michael tried to extract himself from his admirers in order to make the committee meeting.

"Hey guys, I have to get to a meeting in the auditorium."

Emma took his hand. "I'll show you the way."

"Your name is Emma, right?"

Emma nodded and smiled excitedly. "You remember my name?"

"How could I forget the name of such a charming guide?"

As he followed her, the young students begin shouting out questions as to whether he knew various celebrities and who is dating whom and what is it like to be on stage with thousands watching you. Michael abruptly stopped and turned to the students and raised his right hand in a halt gesture.

"Look kids, I promised to help the school on the fund-raising concert and a promise is a promise."

A chorus by some of the girls started.

"Don't make Michael late."

Michael faced the girls and put his finger over his lips and they were quieted but no one wanted to leave and the small mob continued to follow him to the auditorium.

Inside the auditorium, Sophia was already in the meeting

on the stage with four other teachers including Matteo, as well as the Preside (Principal) of the school and Anna, the student counselor. As Sophia called the meeting to order, a noise in the corridor got louder and louder. The doors flew open, and Emma came rushing in with Michael, followed by a crowd of students.

Matteo yelled out at the interruption.

"Che diavolo sta succedendo?" (What the hell is going on?)

Michael realized he had disrupted the meeting. He could see on their faces that his entrance with all the students had annoyed some members and embarrassed Sophia.

Michael put up his hands in a surrender gesture. "Sorry, the students were showing me the way."

The Preside stood up and glared at the students who were still talking and giggling.

"Se non vuoi finire in punizione o prendere una nota sul registro...vai subito a casa senza fare storie." (If you don't want detention or a mark on your record...go home now and do it quietly.)

The students stopped their chatter and nodded, then gave Michael a thumbs-up gesture and scurried out of the auditorium. Michael straightened his jacket and walked with bravado up the aisle and jumped onto the stage. As he did, he turned to look out over the empty seats and smiled, remembering his own high school auditorium. After Sophia introduced Michael as a volunteer member of the committee, he went to each member of the committee. He stopped to shake hands with the men and kissed the women on both cheeks. Matteo grabbed his hand and began squeezing it very hard to demonstrate his superior strength. Michael returned the grip equally strong which surprised Matteo, who then released his grip quickly. Michael looked him in the eye and smiled.

"Matteo, I understand from Sophia that you are also the wrestling coach. I did some freestyle wrestling in high school, would love to talk about it when you have some time."

Matteo muttered under his breath "Che paravento," (wise guy) and sat down.

Sophia watched the two men curiously, wondering what they said to each other.

Michael sat quietly with a small writing pad and listened to the members report on their part in the fundraising concert. He ignored the sullen looks that Matteo was sending his way. He took notes on things he thought were important, listing the three things he thought were serious issues and needed immediate action. During the presentations, Michael noticed that Anna, the attractive student counselor kept smiling at him. At the end of the discussions, Sophia summarized the open issues that she thought were most important.

"Based on your reports, these are the urgent things we have to solve. The first one is that the budget for the project is projected to be short by about twenty thousand Euros. It also appears that a few of the entertainers we counted on wouldn't commit. The last concern was that the lighting and sound company we hired to handle the staging backed out because they had a better paying offer. These are the biggest problems needing our immediate attention."

The members all nodded agreement.

Michael raised his hand.

Sophia looked surprised.

"Yes, Michael?"

Michael stood up. "If I might... My manager once told me there are no problems, only opportunities to solve difficult issues, which can come up on any important project."

All eyes were then on him, including a curious look from Sophia.

"Here's how I think maybe I can help. On the shortfall, I will take it upon myself to get a donation to fill the budget gap. I will also call some of my Italian and other European entertainer contacts and get commitments for the day of the fundraiser. As to the technical staging, I will ask my road manager to solve that one for us. He knows everybody in the business."

The members smiled and clapped politely. Anna started clapping enthusiastically and received a curious glance from Sophia. Everyone seemed relieved by Michael's promise to help except for Matteo. Sophia gave Michael an approving nod.

"Bravo Michael, that was a generous offer. The committee thanks you."

Michael nodded with a slight smile. "It will be my pleasure to do this."

After the meeting, Michael escorted Sophia to her car. As she was getting in the car, she stopped and clasped his hand with hers.

"If you're able to solve those problems, I mean opportunities, it would be a lifesaver for this fundraising effort. It would make my day, that's for sure."

Michael laughed. "I'll tell Clint that you borrowed his line the next time I see him. If we're going to pull this thing off, we need to get together this Saturday and make all the plans to have it happen. I'll make some calls tonight and brief you."

Sophia shook Michael's hand very businesslike. "Thank you. I'll look forward to your report."

She then kissed him on both cheeks and quickly got into her car and drove off.

Michael stood there for a minute in thought then smiled broadly and turned to walk to his car with a new bounce in his step, only to be confronted by Matteo, who blocked his way.

"Don't think because you are a celebrity you can come here and take my Sophia from me."

Michael put up his hands defensively while his face reflected his annoyance with Matteo.

"Look, Matteo. I'm not here to take anyone away from

anyone. Sophia is a childhood friend of mine and a mature woman with a mind of her own. How you and she feel about each other is between you and her. I'm only here to help with the concert. I'd love to chat, but I must get back to my work at my grandfather's winery and do what I promised at the meeting. By the way, I am sincere about talking to you about your school's wrestling program."

Matteo thought for a few seconds. "Maybe I'll teach you a few lessons."

"I bet you could."

Matteo still was blocking Michael from getting to his car.

Michael brushed past Matteo, pushing him back hard with his shoulder. Before Matteo could react, Michael drove off. Matteo stood for a minute wondering why the pampered celebrity wasn't intimidated by him.

In a telephone meeting with Sophia between her scheduled classes the next day, Michael reported on his progress.

"On the contribution, twenty thousand Euros was sent by electronic transfer to your finance person to cover the budget shortfall. It's a contribution from my grandfather's vineyard. I was able to get commitments from several of the Italian talents that were on your list and am waiting to hear on some others. I also spoke to my road manager, Billy. He said he'd take care of arranging all the staging, lighting and sound requirements."

"Michael, that's really good news. Could you come over tonight for a short meeting?"

"Sure."

Michael and Sophia met in the office of her father at the Mariano farmhouse to discuss the concert. The sparks of old feelings were becoming evident to both, though it appeared from their restrained body language and conversation that neither wanted to act on them.

Just as they were wrapping up, Michele came in. When he

saw Michael, he smiled.

"Mamma, Michael si chiama come me... Gli sto insegnando a giocare a calcio." (Mother, Michael has the same name as me... I'm teaching him to play soccer.)

Sophia looked over at Michael, surprised, then turned to her son. "That's very nice Michele. Mr. Ventura needs all the help you can give him. He only knows how to put the basketball in a hoop."

Michele went up to Michael and took his hand.

"You show me how to put the big ball in the basket?"

"In fact, I'll show both of you. I think your Mamma may also need help to put it in the basket."

"You can tell Mr. Ventura that I was on the college women's team that won the city championship if he's interested in a contest."

Maria called out for them to hear. "Sophia, your man is here!"

Michael gave Sophia a quizzical look.

"It's only Matteo. We had a dinner date.

Maria escorted Matteo into the office without knocking and interrupted the conversation. When Matteo saw that Michael was there, he bristled and became officious.

"Sophia! Did you forget we had plans?"

"No, of course not. Michael was letting me know that the three commitments he made that have been accomplished."

Michael got up and grasped Matteo's arm with a friendly grip. "Good to see you, Matteo. I have to get back to my duties. You two have a nice dinner.

As Michael reached the front door, he turned.

"Sophia! When you have time, call me so we can coordinate the social media campaign to fill the seats and raise the funds. I'm going to call one of my affluent friends to see if I can get us a big donation."

As Sophia left for her dinner date, Michael's face reflected unhappiness with Matteo's interruption and that he used the term "my Sophia."

That night, Michael put in a call to his friend Jim Litman.

"Hey, Jim. Hope things are going well, and I need a big favor. I'm helping a local school here to raise funds to build a science lab and a computer room. We're going to give a concert in Siena, and I was hoping you could help us reach the goal with a donation from your philanthropic foundation, or perhaps one of your European companies."

"Michael, so good to hear from you. I have to go into a meeting in a few minutes. Email me the details and an invitation to that concert. I'll take care of it. Sounds like my friend is himself again and doing a good deed. Sorry, but I've got to go now! Call you when it's set up, we can chat then."

A week later the committee met to finalize the program. Michael was happy to report that the plan for the technical staging of the concert was proceeding in a professional manner as Billy liked to be efficient and fast. The Preside and Anna reported how pleased they were with the men that Billy sent and thanked Michael for arranging it. Michael stopped them with a raised hand.

"That kind of work is way above my pay grade. You should thank Billy who knows his business. I only made a telephone call."

The Preside put his hand on Michael's shoulder. "I wish I could make such telephone calls."

Everyone laughed. Michael sheepishly looked pleased.

Later in the meeting, Michael received a text message then reported that his friend Jim committed to matching all funds donated to the school through his European subsidary. The committee members began clapping and thanked him for all the things he had done. When the meeting ended, Matteo quickly went over to Sophia to distract her from talking to Michael. Getting the hint, Michael shook hands with the others. Sophia noticed when Anna went out of her way to kiss Michael goodbye on both cheeks then lingered to have a conversation out of earshot. As they all left the building, Michael's student admirers and some young female fans from the village surrounded Michael. Matteo kept close to Sophia who was waiting for the crowd to clear. Sophia's face reflected her dismay at all the attention that her old friend got from young women.

Michael finally was able to untangle himself from his admirers and started back to talk to Sophia, who felt uncomfortable with Matteo gripping her arm and hovering so close. It was obvious that he was staking out his territory and she was annoyed.

"Matteo! You're hurting my arm."

She forcefully took his hand off her arm and moved toward Michael. Matteo flared and kept next to her. Michael, not realizing what was happening, caught up to them and tapped Matteo on his arm.

"Matteo, I think Jim's commitment is going to make your science lab project a definite reality. If you have time, I'd like to take you both to dinner and celebrate."

Michael extended his hand. Matteo used the gesture to grip Michael and turn him suddenly. He then used a wrestling inside leg kick to drop him to the ground, causing a gasp from Sophia and others who witnessed it. Michael was more embarrassed than hurt physically by the unexpected aggression. Matteo reached over to help Michael get up with a sly smile on his face.

"Sorry. I expected you would know that move."

Michael was fuming and ready to fight. When he saw that Sophia was extremely upset, he decided to diffuse the situation.

"That was a great move. I haven't seen the leg kick drop done so smoothly before. Why don't you show me more of your moves when we're both prepared?"

"I could teach you a lesson when you have time."

"I'd like that. Sometime over the weekend, okay?"

Sophia was both upset at Matteo and mystified by Michael's reaction. She concluded it must be a "guy" thing and decided to let them settle it on their own but would deal with Matteo in her own way.

The following night, Sophia showed up unexpectedly at the Ventura farmhouse and was greeted warmly by Manuela.

"What a pleasant surprise!"

Manuela kissed Sophia and gave her a hug. Sophia returned the affection.

"I came to see how Aurelio is doing."

"He seems to get stronger each day."

Sophia smiled warmly. "That's good news. I also wanted to thank Michael person-ally for all his help in making this concert a success. His friend is even going to match all the funds donated to the projects to ensure that we reach our goal. I don't think this event would even happen without his help. His experience has been invaluable, and his contacts made all the difference."

Manuela went to get her jacket. "Come with me. He just went out to show the winery to a woman from your committee named Anna."

Taken off guard by the news, Sophia was a little flustered. "Yes, of course. Anna is a devoted student counselor and a wonderful person. I didn't know she was coming tonight."

Manuela put on her jacket. "Let's go join them. I'm sure that Michael would love to see you."

Sophia thought for a minute. "No, let Anna have some time alone with Michael. I can talk to him another time and I should get home anyway, promised to help my mother with dinner."

As Sophia left, Manuela shrugged then saw Aurelio in the doorway.

"That was a little strange."

"Didn't you notice her reaction when you told Sophia that another woman was with Michael?"

"Ah...I guess the last one to know is the mother."

Chapter 15

MIXED MESSAGES

The next evening Michael called Sophia.

"Could we get together tonight and meet by the gate?"

Sophia was hesitant then nodded to herself. Why not?

"Sure, give me ten minutes."

Michael was waiting as she arrived

"Mom said you came by last night. Why didn't you come and join us? I was only at the winery showing Anna how it worked. She thought some of the students might be interested in careers in agriculture."

Sophia smiled. "That probably is a good idea. I also think Anna may have other ideas of her own and I thought you should not have an old friend hanging around."

"Okay, I know where this is going. Sure, it is a bit flattering for a guy to think an intelligent, attractive young woman would find him interesting but I'm really focusing on other things...like the concert, keeping the winery going and what I should be doing to get my career on track again. However, to set your mind at ease, Anna was a perfect gentleman and didn't try to take advantage of poor little me."

Sophia burst out laughing and touched his arm. "Sorry, I'm only a country girl who saw on those videos of your concerts lots of beautiful women grabbing you and hugging you. I just didn't want to interfere with your social life or inhibit you from pursuing relationships."

"I appreciate that, but please know that I'm aware of the difference between what happens to me as a celebrity and things that happen in my real life. My reality became a nightmare when Louisa got so sick and then died. I cared deeply for her. I really thought we could beat the cancer like she did as a teenager. I felt like I failed her."

Sophia reached out and took both his hands. "Michael, you are a successful man, not God. I know from Manuela that you were there for her right to the end. A lesser man would have backed away. I was so sorry when I heard. It must have been a terrible thing for you to go through and for you to watch someone you love die. We sent a Mass card, but we should have been there for you. You're not the only one with regrets."

Michael sighed. "I guess life sometimes is like riding a roller coaster. We're up at the top one day and at the bottom the next, with lots of twists and turns to knock you around. Louisa was such a kind and loving person and she died much too soon."

Michael began tearing up. Sophia put her arms around his neck. Tears were running down their cheeks as she held him close. Michael held her tight. His eyes were closed.

"Who's there?"

Pietro's voice came from a distance and the two friends separated quickly like two kids caught doing something wrong.

"It's only me," Michael said, quickly wiping his eyes

"I was just talking to our neighbor. Be right there."

Sophia had instinctively ducked down. She grinned at the

situation and waved goodbye to Michael then quickly and quietly went through the connecting gate and back toward the Mariano farmhouse.

The next morning Michael was standing outside the Ventura farmhouse on the phone with his friend Billy, who reported that he had already scoped out the facility for staging, sound and lighting. He wanted to reassure his friend that everything would be up and running on time. Michael thanked him, put down his cell, then thought for a minute and called Gerry.

"Gerry, it's me. I want to get back to touring next year. I miss singing, I miss my fans, I miss the action and the craziness... Hey, I even miss you. I've been looking at some new songs to include. After the fundraiser in Siena, I'm all yours. I need a big favor. Looks like we aren't going home for a long time. Our pet Deedee is now staying with a married cousin and her family. If I text you the information, could you make contact and arrangements to get DeeDee here?"

Gerry punched the air silently.

"I'm on it. We'll make it a comeback tour to remember, and I'll get DeeDee to Italy if I have to buy her a first-class ticket."

Michael laughed. "That is an image. She would drive the flight attendant nuts barking for treats."

When he hung up the phone, Michael walked outside, took a deep breath and started singing an upbeat song, "Feeling Good," which was originally written by Anthony Newley and Lesley Bricusse for a musical theater production that played on the West End and on Broadway.

Manuela, who was at her bedroom window, smiled hearing her son feeling so positive. She tapped on the window and Michael looked up to see her giving a thumbs up, which made him blow her a kiss and start singing again.

Energized by being busy and enjoying the beauty of the

Tuscan countryside, he began to replay his encounter with Sophia and think positively again. His cell rang. It was Sophia.

"Hi, what's up?"

"I must go to Florence and pick something up from my aunt's store. I remember when we were kids you said you always wanted to check out the city and thought you might like to come with me tomorrow."

"Sure, that sounds great, what time did you want to leave?"

"Can we go early, about seven? It will take almost two hours. Is that too early?"

"No, that's perfect. I've been getting up at six lately. I'll pick you up. My rental car has been sitting too much and needs a good long run."

"That would be wonderful. I don't like going alone and prefer not to drive long distances by myself. See you in the morning."

Michael walked over to check on the car and saw that his beautiful silver BMW was covered with a dulling dust. He shrugged, disappointed about its less than sparkling condition. He drove it over to the garage and washed it until it was in showroom condition. When he was finished, he admired his handy work and felt good that he was ready for his trip with Sophia.

The next morning Michael pulled up to the Mariano farmhouse right at seven am sharp. Before he could get out of the car, Sophia ran out and scooted into the passenger seat.

"Wow, this is one beautiful automobile. It must cost a fortune to rent."

"I think my manager Gerry was so happy that I left my house, he wanted to encourage me to get out more. He arranged to rent this amazing vehicle."

Sophia was feeling the leather seat. "You tell your Gerry I feel like a princess just being in it."

"Then it's worth every Euro it costs to rent, because you're sitting in it make me really feel like a celebrity. Tell me, what is this important thing we have to pick up in Florence?"

"To be truthful, it isn't that important. My mission is to pick up two dresses that my Aunt Angela, who is a well-known designer, made for my mother and me for my Cousin Tina's wedding. Mom is a worrier and didn't want to wait for the shop to deliver it."

"Isn't driving to Florence a long trip just to pick up dresses?"

"Maybe, but it is also an excuse to go there and show the city off to you."

"Then thank your talented aunt for me. Florence, here we come"

Sophia looked across at Michael and cleared her throat then spoke quickly. "I know it's a big ask, but would you like to be my plus one at the wedding? It's in two weeks and it won't be a fancy kind of reception. Tina and Tommaso are very young and don't have much money. I understand they'll get married in the village church and have a modest reception. Actually, it will be catered by her maid of honor at her godfather's small hotel just down the street. My mother said they won't have a band, just an old fashion record player that her friend is lending the family."

"Sounds like it should be fun like in the old days. Of course, I'd love to come. When you add may name, could you just tell them you're bringing one of your old friends so someone doesn't mention it to the media, or the paparazzi will make a spectacle of their wedding. I've been lucky so far staying under their radar."

"I totally understand. I will do that and thank you for saying yes."

As they drove through the beautiful Tuscan countryside Michael and Sophia reminisced about their childhood escapades. As they talked, Sophia smiled then teased.

"You know I still remember when we watched the Palio race, and you had to lean against me to see the race and I didn't know what I felt."

Michael cringed. "Don't remind me. That was more than a little embarrassing for me. Blame it on teenage hormones."

Sophia laughed. "Just so you know, when I told my more world-wise older cousin Vittoria about what happened, she said it was a sign you liked me."

Michael cleared his throat. "Well, that part was true...but for a naive fourteen-year-old trying to make a good impression on a girl he really liked, not such a good thing. I was so embarrassed, I avoided coming to see you because I didn't think you would ever talk to me again. Then the call about my dad's accident changed everything and my mom and I never returned together. The next few years seemed to pass in a flash. When I was a sophomore in high school, a neighbor girl invited me to a dance at her Catholic high school. When we were in a slow dance close together, a Nun came over and put a long ruler between us and said, 'Please leave six inches for the Holy Ghost.' The neighbor girl had no idea what she meant but after our experience, I understood."

Sophia put her hand over her mouth to cover a laugh. "That's what I should have had at the Palio...a long ruler."

Michael just shook his head in amusement, focusing on the road as they entered the ramp onto the Autostrada, then responded with a self-deprecating grin. "When I was fourteen, you wouldn't need anything very long."

Sophia shook off the meaning with her own amused reaction then became more serious. "If my cousin Vittoria was right and you liked me, then why didn't I hear from you after you left without saying goodbye? That one letter you did send made me hope there would be a follow-up. Do you know, I even took English lessons so the next time you came we could talk more easily? I studied your language in college so I could teach English. I remember after we started playing together on your first visit, I thought I was going to be your girlfriend. To be honest, I was a very upset teenager and angry with you when you stopped coming to see me."

Michael nodded that he understood. "My only excuse is that I was a kid and when my dad died, my world became a dark place for me. You wrote those kind letters, but I had no idea what to say. I wish that things had been different, and I was more mature. I did try to call you when I came to see Aurelio. The first time, I was performing in Milan and had a day off. I flew down to see him. He suggested I give you a call and I did. Your mom told me you had just graduated from university and went with your girlfriends to a beach resort I think south of Rome."

"It was Sabaudia. I remember we were all so wound up, we wanted to relax on a sandy beach and unwind."

"I was really happy and proud that you finished college. I did okay in high school but when my career took off, that ended any plans to go to college. The next time I called your mom, she said you were away for the whole summer on a cruise. I think she said to the Caribbean."

"That was on my honeymoon with Lorenzo. That was the first time we spent a lot of time together. Lorenzo and I met in college; he was this very handsome, attentive guy and as you say in English, he swept me off my feet. We were married two years after we graduated. He later became very wealthy after his grandfather left him a great deal of money. Between his looks and spending money freely on jewelry and parties, he attracted the attention of lots of beautiful women. I know you do because you are very good-looking, talented and a very popular performer. He, on the other, really loved flirting with them. Unfortunately for our marriage, as I found out later, he had three mistresses stashed in apartments in different cities.

He managed to cheat because I naively believed him when he told me he was helping his father, who is a big wine exporter. The only thing he was really helping was himself. Having a wife and child were not his priority and he let me know it."

"I'm so sorry you had to go through all that. I guess fate caused our lives to go in different directions. When my dad died, we were completely in shock; everything changed for us. My mom and I had to find work to pay bills and our life was very different and extremely difficult. The truth is, it was only after the insurance people finally settled on the accident case years later that we were able to do things as before. By then I was trying to find myself and what I should be doing for the future. When I started singing professionally at eighteen, I was constantly on the road touring or in the studio recording. It was because of all the traveling that I lost a girlfriend I thought was the one. When I met Louisa, who was a violinist in the orchestra, she took charge after each concert ended as if she and I were involved just to protect me. We became good friends at first but over time we became more than buddies. She was a wonderful caring person. You would have liked her. It's only since I had to step up to help with the vineyard because Aurelio was so sick, and you asked me to help on the fundraiser, that I began to be me again. It was not only the satisfaction of helping to raise money for a good cause, but I also began to feel our old connection again. I wanted to respect that you were in a relationship with Matteo. Now I want you to know I do have feelings for you that are more than a neighborly friendship."

Sophia smiled and gave his arm a squeeze. "Maybe neighbors have feelings too. Speaking of Matteo, I was very angry he tripped you the other day and I told him so. What was that all about?"

"Jealousy can make people do things you wouldn't expect."

"Your reaction was different than I expected."

"My first reaction was to kick his butt. Then I thought, the success of the fundraiser depends on your committee working together. I decided to handle it, let's say in a more gentlemanly way."

"On behalf of the fundraiser, I thank you. If it were me, I would have kicked Mateo in a place he would not forget."

"What I don't get is that your rural school has a top-notch Greco-Roman wrestling program. I understand that wrestling in Italy as a sport is usually found in large cities and private academies. Not in small rural high schools. How did that happen?"

"Mateo single-handedly pushed for the program because he was trained in a private academy school and considered one of the best in the sport. I think you call it freestyle. He told me he wanted our students to have the opportunity to learn the sport instead of just rough street fighting. I think he also hoped someday one of his students would be good enough to compete in the Olympics for Italy."

"Impressive. By the way it's also called Folkstyle in the US. I'm meeting him tomorrow for a wrestling lesson. Should be interesting and possibly humbling."

"Be careful. I need you presentable in two weeks as my plus one, which I said was my old friend."

Michael laughed and reached for Sophia's hand and held it gently. "As your old friend, I will do my best not to embarrass you."

She smiled and squeezed back then put his hand back on the steering wheel. "Mr. Ventura, now please keep both hands on the wheel and eyes on the road. There are important dresses waiting for us."

Michael made an exaggerated gesture of gripping the steering wheel very tightly and being dramatic about making eye contact with the road ahead.

Sophia couldn't stop smiling as she leaned back and closed

her eyes.

Michael was parked outside a fancy-dress store in the business district of Florence. He watched as Sophia came out and excitedly carried the plastic-wrapped dresses, which she carefully laid out in the backseat. Michael started the car.

"Okay Ms. Mariano, what's your pleasure?"

"To park this chariot and see central Firenze by bicycle, of course."

For the next several hours they toured the main tourist areas: The Duomo, Baptistery of St. John, Piazza de Michelangelo and a panoramic view of the city, Uffizi Palace and Gallery, Piazza della Signoria, which had a copy of Michelangelo's statue of David.

At the Duomo and Uffizi Palace, Michael was recognized and had to sign autographs while an amused Sophia watched with mixed feelings at her chauffeur's celebrity. That was until a beautiful young woman became a little too attentive, slipping Michael a card. Sophia moved quickly and took the card.

"Mr. Ventura has to leave for an important meeting in Siena. We thank you so much for being a wonderful fan. I'll make sure we send you an autographed picture."

Sophia took Michael's arm and pulled him toward the bicycles. "Mr. Ventura, you will be late for your appointment if we don't start back now."

As they left the bicycle rental place and headed to the car, Michael stopped to face Sophia and take her arm at the elbow.

"What was that all about with my fan?"

"I thought if we don't keep moving, we'll be arriving in the dark."

"You do know the car is equipped with headlights and is drivable at night."

"Yes, in fact, I did know that they were equipping cars for night driving."

"What I didn't know is that you have autographed pictures

of me to send to my fans. You are full of surprises."

Sophia's face made a frown and she hit him in the shoulder with a playful punch. "If you don't get in the car, Mr. Ventura, you may get to know something you wouldn't like."

Michael laughed. "Now there's my old friend Sophia. When we first met you threatened me because you thought I was trespassing on my own grandfather's property."

"I remember it was you who threatened to call the police on a poor sweet nine-year-old."

"I was only kidding. You told your mom to do it."

"What's a girl to do when she doesn't understand the foreign boy yelling at her?"

"Touché...our folks must've had a few laughs out of all that drama."

Sophia nodded knowingly and smiled. "My mom reminded me of that when I was annoyed you didn't answer my letters."

When they were back in the car, Michael started the powerful engine, looked across at Sophia who was daydreaming, then sped off, causing her to fall back in her seat. Michael reached for her hand and squeezed it. Sophia smiled and squeezed back then put his hand back on the steering wheel.

"Both hands on the wheel."

As they drove, Michael became thoughtful.

"I heard that your ex doesn't visit his son very often. How does Michele deal with that?"

Sophia became very pensive and sad. "That's been a terrible situation. Last time I asked Michele about his dad, he said 'The next time my dad comes, I'm going to say I don't talk to strangers.'"

Michael shook his head, somewhat shocked. "Whoa, that's one heavy response. The depth of it is both impressive that such a young boy would make it and upsetting that he had to."

"Tell me about it."

"Why was your son named Michele, is there a family connection?"

"Not really, I liked the name. It reminded me of an old friend from my childhood."

Michael became thoughtful and looked straight ahead at the road. Sophia became pensive and began looking out of the window at the countryside. As they drove, both continued in silence. Both were thinking about their past and the reasons why destiny took them on different paths and then ended up here. Michael looked over at Sophia. At that moment, her eyes opened, and she smiled warmly at him. He suddenly felt a calm that he hadn't experienced in a long time. He smiled as he thought about an old love song, "This Can't Be Love," which he sang at his concerts and which was an old favorite of Nat King Cole. He started to sing the lyrics in n his head while his mouth was silently mouthing the words.

Sophia opened her eyes and looked over at Michael, wondering why his lips were moving and no sound was coming out.

"What's going on? Are you rehearsing a new song?"

"Something like that. Actually, it's an old one. I began thinking about a song called 'This Can't Be Love,' which I like to perform at my concerts. It was originally written in 1938 by Rogers and Hart for a Broadway show. The great Nat King Cole also covered it as part of an album *For Two in Love*, which he recorded in the 1950s."

"Sounds like a nice song. Please sing it for me!"

When Michael began singing with feeling, Sophia reacted. Michael glanced over at her lovingly.

"I love to look in your eyes."

Sophia put her hand over her eyes, so he didn't see her tears.

Chapter 16

FINDING ANSWERS

Manuela heard the car drive up and looked out the window to see Michael jump out of the car with a spring in his step, which made her smile.

She went to the door and onto the porch.

"I trust you had an enjoyable tour of Florence."

"It was a beautiful place. Took some pictures with my cell. We can look at them after I take a quick shower."

"That would be nice. Did Sophia get her package okay?"

"No problem, everything went great. I have a thing at the school in the morning, but I'm thinking that maybe we should invite the Mariano family for a Sunday dinner like in the old days. I know your dad likes their company. Oh, I almost forgot. Sophia invited me to be a plus one at her cousin Tina's wedding in Lucca. I may have to ask you about the wedding protocols around here."

Manuela's eyes reflected her surprise, then a wry smile foreshadowed her response. "I always thought you were number one, now my son is also going to be a plus one."

"Now you're not taking this seriously."

"Sorry, I couldn't resist a good quip. Seriously, family is very important to the Mariano's so inviting you was a big deal. I remember when you sang at your cousin's wedding in Long Island and how much they appreciated it."

"You think that would be something I should do?"

Manuela touched his arm. "That's above a mother's pay grade. I will call Maria about dinner tomorrow. Should I also invite their daughter Sophia as well?"

As he rushed by his mom, Michael gave her a "*now you're being a wise ass*" look, but he just said "Definitely!"

On Sunday morning, Michael was up early doing warm up exercises to get himself ready for Matteo's lesson. He knew he was not going to be at his best when he realized how long it had been since he wrestled in high school. He thought about canceling but decided to settle it one way or another.

When Michael arrived at the school, Matteo was waiting at the entrance. Without greeting Michael, he ushered him into the building.

"Matteo, could we talk before we do this?"

"I don't think we have much to say to each other. You don't respect that Sophia and I are seeing each other. I called her house yesterday and know you took her on a trip to Firenze in your fancy car."

"That's right. Sophia had promised me a long time ago she would show me Florence and was only making good on that. I was not trying to take her away. I told her I wanted to be your friend because Sophia is my old friend, and we have to work together on the fundraiser."

Matteo shook his head, confused by Michael's words. "Let's just do what we're here for."

"Okay."

Matteo led the way to the locker room and the two men changed quickly. Matteo ushered Michael through a corridor into another room. Michael looked around, very impressed that the rural school had such a well-equipped training facility for a freestyle wrestling program.

"Matteo! This is a terrific set up. You should be congratulated on organizing such a top-notch place to train your students."

Matteo was taken by surprise by the compliment but showed he was pleased with a slight smile. "We do our best. Our team is doing so well, we were even invited a few days ago to compete in Bologna. The Preside said they could spare a little from the general budget but not enough. The school's limited sport's budget is mostly for the calcio (soccer) team."

"I'll tell you what; let me know how much you need, and I'll make up the shortfall. My music teacher took me under her wing when we were having a difficult time after my dad was killed in a traffic accident. Her interest in my learning the basics was one of the reasons I ended up in a career in music. Challenging your students to compete at a higher level may not earn them a career in the sport, but it will give them confidence in themselves."

Matteo was completely taken off guard by Michael's offer. "I...must thank you for the team. They were disappointed we might not go. Your offer should get us a quick approval."

"Okay, now that's settled, we get on with the lesson."

Matteo was having second thoughts about his reason for having it out with Michael. "Yes, of course. We can learn a few techniques from each other."

During the next half hour, Matteo taught Michael an aggressive "head and arm pin" technique as well as a very effective "head and arm throw" move. While Michael tried to defend against his more experienced opponent with a "leg ride technique" he had learned and even a usually effective half-nelson trying to pin him, Matteo was able to thwart his efforts. By time they were finished and totally exhausted, Michael had been pinned twice and knew when to stop. After the two men began to breathe normally again, Michael extended his hand with a slight smile.

"That was a great lesson for me, to never take on someone in a sport who is much better at it than you are."

Matteo laughed and shook his hand. "If you ever want to work out, give me a call. I need someone like you to keep me from losing my edge, but don't get too good or you will bruise my ego."

Michael thought about the offer then nodded. "I may take you up on that when things quiet down."

The two showered and dressed in silence, then quickly left the building together and gave each other a slight wave on the way to their cars.

Later that day, Sophia and her family were getting ready to leave to go to the Ventura dinner when the door chimes rang. Sophia went to answer the door.

"I'll get it."

She opened the door to find Matteo carrying a bouquet of roses. Before she could react, he handed her the flowers.

"I was out driving, and remembered I owed you an apology from the other day. I'd offer to take you to dinner, but our friend Michael told me you were having dinner at the Ventura vineyard."

Sophia was shocked by what Matteo said about Michael being our friend. "These are beautiful. Thank you, and I'm happy that you and Michael are okay. Why don't I call the Venturas? They're always happy to have another guest."

"No, please don't. I just wanted to tell you I'm sorry for my boorish behavior. Give my regards to your parents. I'll see you at school."

Matteo turned and quickly went to his car and drove away. Sophia watched him leave; very confused that he called Michael his friend and grateful that he said it.

Maria tapped Sophia's shoulder. She and Francesco were dressed and ready to leave. Maria looked curiously at her holding a bouquet of flowers.

"Are you bringing those with you?"

"Oh, Matteo stopped by."

Both nodded and just said "Ah!"

Maria took them from her daughter to smell them.

"They're beautiful. Let's give them to Manuela."

The mixed Italian-English dinner conversation at the Ventura farmhouse was lively and sometimes loud between Aurelio, Maria, Francesco and Manuela, while Michael and Sophia moved to Aurelio's office to discuss the concert. Sophia was open about her concerns that things might go wrong at the last minute. Michael grasped her hand.

"Stop worrying so much. I'm sure the talent will show up and the technical support team will make it all work. I'm confident that it will be successful."

Sophia's facial expression reflected her more cautious outlook. "I hope so. It's been my experience that unexpected glitches always seem to come up."

"Of course, they can and often do, but if they do, we'll deal with them. Like most performance events, the audience only experiences what they see and hear. Minor flaws are tolerated as long as the main event is good."

Sophia gripped his hand back and leaned toward him. "You are always so positive about these things, probably because you have much more experience."

Michael shrugged and smiled. "At my concerts, I always try to do my best and trust that everybody else will do theirs. Of course there have been glitches, but the audience generally aren't aware of the small ones and seem to tolerate the big ones as part of the experience. By the way, I heard your mom tell mine that Matteo stopped by. Did he say anything about our wrestling session?"

"For some strange reason, he referred to you as our friend then apologized for the other day at school and presented me with the roses we just gave to Manuela. Either you somehow bewitched him or hurt him so badly his brain was damaged."

"Nothing so dramatic. We met to wrestle it out this morning. I found that Matteo is a great wrestler and easily beat me fair and square. After we finished, he said he would help me train and I said I'd help his team go to the wrestling meet in Bologna. What can I tell you? He's very good at the sport as I found out the hard way. My ego was a little shaken, but my brain didn't get stirred and no visible bruises for when I show up for the wedding."

"I guess I'll never fully understand men."

Michael reached over and took both of Sophia's hands. "All women must do is keep us full of the food we like and appreciate it when we try to help. There may be other things better discussed in private."

A blush then a broad smile broke out on Sophia's beautiful face. "Now that is a talk I would love to hear."

Manuela's voice came from the next room. "Michael! Could you help me carry something upstairs?"

Michael put his hand up for Sophia to hold off on their conversation. "Be right there."

As Michael rushed out, Sophia was about to say something when Aurelio came into the room.

"Mr. Ventura, it's so good to see you back on your feet. I wanted to personally thank you for the donation to make up our shortfall. It was very generous."

Aurelio shifted his eyes toward where Michael exited. "I'm not the one you should thank, but he wouldn't want you to know."

"I should have guessed."

"Please don't say anything. He'd be embarrassed."

Michael came back into the room and saw Sophia and

Aurelia talking together. "Hey, you two. How about a coffee and a piece of Tiramisu from Taverna DeCecco in Siena?"

Aurelio took Sophia's arm to escort her.

"If you have tiramisu from that place, you don't have to ask us twice."

Chapter 17

DOING GOOD DEEDS

The next time Michael arrived at the school for a fundraising meeting he was immediately surrounded by his student admirers. Emma touched his elbow.

"Michael, I am such a big fan of your style of music, like my mom and grandfather. Would you sing a duet with me at our school recital? Ms. Mariano will be there."

Michael was amused by her pointed reference to Sophia and intrigued because the girl was being assertive enough to ask him.

"Emma, I'm flattered but shouldn't you ask a fellow student since it's a school function?"

"With you there, everyone will come to hear us, and I won't be nervous like I usually am."

"I see...when is it?"

"Friday...it's at eleven o'clock in the place you have those meetings. I would love to sing one of those old songs with you. My nonno plays them at home, and he'll be coming with my mom."

Michael gave her a long look. "How can I refuse two big fans and a grandfather? Did you know my nonno was the one who got me started?"

"I remember that in an interview you did...I guess we are both fortunate."

"Okay. We'll do the duet, but I have two conditions. We will sing the light-hearted song 'Feeling Good,' and you have to be there at ten o'clock sharp so we can rehearse."

Emma jumped up and down and gave him a big hug. "I will learn the lyrics and practice it every day so I can sing it with you on Friday."

"Now can I go to the meeting, so they don't kick me off?"

Her friends were so excited they surrounded Michael and hugged him. Michael extracted himself and walked quickly into the school and down the hall to the auditorium. In his rush not to be late, he didn't realize that Emma's friends were quietly following him as he entered the auditorium.

Clearing his throat loudly, the Preside stood up and stared down at the students.

"Ragazze...penso che il signor Ventura possa gestire l'incontro da solo." (Girls...I think Mr. Ventura can handle the meeting on his own.)

As the girls retreated, they blew kisses, and some yelled out loud.

"See you Friday, Michael."

The Preside was shocked by the girls addressing a mature man in such a familiar way. "Mr. Ventura, what is that all about? These are underage girls."

Michael shrugged, a little embarrassed. "Hey. I'm not that guy. I only promised one of the girls named Emma that I would sing with her at Friday's recital and her friends became a little enthusiastic."

The Preside cleared his throat again. "Oh? That's very generous of you. Emma is normally very shy but has a wonderful singing voice. I'm surprised she would even ask you."

"The reason I agreed was because I wanted to encourage assertiveness. Most young people, including me at that age, are too insecure."

Michael looked over and saw that Sophia was sporting one of her charming wry smiles.

"Mr. Ventura is famous for his popularity with ladies of all ages. We will look forward to his duet with our talented Emma. Now, if no one objects, we should get on with our meeting."

Everyone took their seat as Sophia made eye contact with Michael, nodding her approval of his helping Emma.

At the end of the short meeting to do a final checklist, Sophia stood up.

"If there is no other business to discuss, this meeting is over. Thank you all for your input and help."

Michael followed Matteo, who was moving quickly toward the door. He tapped Matteo on the shoulder. As Michael talked with Matteo, Sophia overheard part of Michael's conversation as she moved closer.

"...I began working on the fundraiser because Sophia is an old friend from childhood...."

Sophia face reflected her hurt as she turned and quickly left.

While the men were still talking, Anna heard the rest of the conversation.

"...but just so we're clear on this, I do care a great deal about Sophia and will do whatever I can to be there for her. I promise not to say anything that interferes with your relationship, but my own feelings for her are my business and not negotiable. It's been great that we can talk like two adults now. I'll check back with you tomorrow about having a beer together. Now I have to get back or my nonno will fire me."

Matteo watched Michael leave and was in deep thought as

Anna put her hand on his shoulder.

"Ciao Matteo...I think we don't understand what's going on with Michael and Sophia because they themselves don't. If you need someone with a friendly ear, let me know."

Matteo was shaken out of his thoughts. When he looked at Anna, he was surprised he never noticed that her eyes were hazel or that she smelled of vanilla.

"Ciao Anna...I believe you may be right and I may take your ear up on the offer."

Anna smiled. "My stomach's favorite dish is cotoletta alla milanese if you're asking. Have a good evening, Matteo."

Matteo smiled broadly and watched as Anna turned to leave. As his eyes followed her out he liked what he saw.

Michael threw himself into his work at the vineyard and winery, working long hours to make sure the operation was successful. After work, he began vocalizing to test his singing range. After practicing for an hour, he stopped to text Sophia.

"Can we get together tonight?"

Sophia responded, "Don't think that's necessary."

Confused, Michael sent her another text. "Okay...let me know if you need me."

Michael wore a concerned look as he sat at the office desk with a file folder to work on balancing the winery's monthly income and expense entries.

Sophia was in her father's office chair. She was staring at a picture of Michael and her as children and whispered loudly to herself.

"Oh Michael, is that all I am to you now? Just an old friend."

On Friday, Michael showed up at ten o'clock for the recital. He was met by the Preside as he entered the auditorium.

"Emma called the music teacher five minutes ago and told her she wasn't feeling well. The teacher thinks she has stage fright and that's why she's not coming. I'm sorry you had to come all the way to find out."

Michael thought for a minute before responding. "Could you get me her cellphone number and her address?"

The Preside took out his cellphone. "Mrs. Garibaldi! Please get me Emma's cellphone number and address...no! right now."

When he received the information, Michael immediately called.

Emma answered in a nervous voice.

"Hi. Who is calling?"

"Emma! This is Michael Ventura. I'm here at the school for the rehearsal."

"Oh Mr. Ventura, I'm so sorry. I was too nervous and didn't want to embarrass you."

Michael made a *whooshing* sound. "I'm coming right over to get you. Be dressed and be ready to leave."

Michael drove fast to Emma's house and knocked on her door. Emma's mother answered and after being surprised that he was there so fast, kissed him on both cheeks.

"Grazie di essere venuto... La mia Emma ti ammira così tanto...siamo grandi fan." (Thank you for coming... My Emma admires you so much...we are big fans.)

"Per cortesia, di 'ad Emma che sono qui." (Please tell Emma I'm here.)

"Per favore entra...dopo che hai chiamato, è andata direttamente in camera sua...Emma scendi! ...c'e' Il Sig. Ventura ... Emma scendi! ...Sig. Ventura è qui!" (Please come in...after you called, she went straight to her room...Emma come down! Mr. Ventura is here.)

Emma came slowly down the stairs all dressed up. "I'm so sorry. You were so kind to let me sing with you. I'm ready now... Do you get nervous before you have to perform before all those people?"

"Someone once told me that emotions are action signals.

Anxiety can produce fear so instead of feeling anxious, I make myself feel excited that I'm actually getting the chance to entertain all those nice folks who came to my concert. It's also an important technique to use at auditions, which can be stressful."

"That sounds like a really good way to deal with things. I'm going to try that."

Michael turned to Mrs. Talarico.

"Per favore, chiama tuo padre e ci vediamo in." ("Please get your father and we'll meet you in the car.)

Michael took Emma's hand and gripped it tight. "We'll rehearse the song as we drive. I'm a professional singer and someday I predict you will be. We honor our commitments, agree?"

Emma nodded. They were opening the car doors as her mom and grandfather came rushing out.

Michael and Emma came on stage as the last performers. The audience of mostly students, teachers and staff went wild as Michael stepped up to the microphone and introduced Emma as his singing partner. They performed "Feeling Good" as a rousing duet with just the rehearsal on the way to the school. Michael was impressed that young Emma was able to do it so well with very little preparation. The old song touched the audience with its positive message and had the audience standing on their feet.

When they came off stage, the Preside gave Emma a big hug and nodded his approval to Michael. Emma was quickly surrounded by her friends as her grandfather had watched with a big smile on his face. As Michael turned, Sophia shook his hand somewhat formally.

"You did a really good deed. Thank you. Emma was amazing, and you did pretty good yourself."

Sophia then turned away to join the excited students and gave Emma a hug. Michael was confused by Sophia's recent businesslike reaction to him.

On Saturday, Michael and Pietro reported to Aurelio.

"The winery is not only doing okay, but the distributor also asked for more product as demand in US and Canada is up 12% from last year. Fortunately, you had increased the grape harvest a few years ago, which will enable us to meet the request this year. It's too bad we didn't have more vineyards to meet the anticipated future growth. We do have capacity in our bottling operation."

Aurelio agreed but was pleased everything was running well and thanked both Pietro and Michael for making it happen.

Pietro put up his hand, "I have to get back to the winery as we are bottling today."

Aurelio waved him away and turned to Michael. "I want to thank you so much for everything. Taking the time to help me was a blessing."

Michael gave his grandfather a hug. "I thank you and this special place. The experience working here with Pietro and at the school with Sophia brought me back from the dark place I was in and made me want to sing again. My manager has already booked me to sing in Rome for a Christmas Eve charity even, which will be televised. He said things were already lining up for a world tour next year."

Aurelio became serious. "That's wonderful, but what will you do about Sophia?"

"Oh, we're all set. Everything is lining up for a successful concert on December 17."

Aurelio took Michael's arm. "Sophia is a wonderful woman. I thought you two would…"

Michael interrupted him. "Sophia is an amazing woman and I care a great deal for her but I'm still dealing with my loss and only recently…anyway, Sophia and I are still figuring our relationship out and the last thing I want is to disappoint her again."

"Michael, let me ask you one question. Would you disappoint her now?"

Michael took his grandfather's arm and looked directly at him. "That is the question, isn't it? I would never want to, but disappointment is a two-way street. Sophia might become disappointed in me and my crazy travel schedule. I lost one close friend from high school because of my constant traveling."

Aurelio held eye contact. "I understand absence can be an issue, but isn't that some-thing for both of you to discuss together?"

Michael, seriously reflecting on his grandfather's words, nodded yes.

"Then go and do something about it. You are a performer and supposed to be good at communicating. So, communicate."

Chapter 18

COMMUNICATING

Michael walked outside the farmhouse and texted Sophia.

"Can we meet at the gate?"

Sophia texted back. "Is there a problem?"

"I hope not. Just want to talk."

The way the message read, made Sophia curious.

"Be there in 10 minutes."

She quickly hung up went into her bedroom and put on a fresh sweater and then went into the bathroom, combed her hair and put on some lipstick.

Michael was waiting at the gate between the two properties as Sophia arrived. He opened the gate and reached out to take Sophia's hand.

"Thanks for coming."

"What's up?"

"Us!"

"I don't understand."

Michael gently took Sophia by her shoulders and brought her close to him.

"Look, we're not naive teens back at the Palio where we didn't understand our hormones or how to express our feelings. I told you before how much I regretted disappearing on you for all those years. Because of that, I really didn't want to mess up your life by interfering in it."

Michael waited for Sophia to react, then watched as she visibly relaxed.

"I thought I told you before. Matteo is a wonderful colleague and usually a very nice person. We would go out occasionally because he was always a gentleman, and I enjoyed talking to an adult after teaching teenagers all day. From my side, that was the extent of our relationship. I do know that he had a different view. When I heard you tell him you were just my old friend the other day, I was hurt because I thought we were more than that."

Michael pulled Sophia to him and held her against him. "I only said that to stop making him so jealous of our working together on the project that could affect our efforts. I also told him I had feelings for you. I want us to be more than friends if you do."

Sophia grinned mischievously. "If I say I do, does that mean we are married in your crazy world?"

Michael laughed. "Even in the music business, there are a few other legal requirements for that to happen. Could we start with a kiss?"

Michael kissed Sophia long and sweet. When they separated, Sophia looked again at Michael seriously.

"One more thing. I see how women react to you. Lorenzo was good looking and a big spender who was able attract individual women. I see how many women react when you are around. I know that you aren't using your celebrity to take advantage, but I do feel inadequate to have to compete."

"How some of my fans feel about me is very different than what a couple might feel based on knowing each other. I read early on there was a neuroscience study about how music and singing can produce oxytocin in a listener's brain. Sometimes it's caused by the emotion of a person's circumstance or the song's lyrics that resonate and create a connection between the performer and a fan. It's called the cuddle hormone for a reason. I do care about the wonderful fans who take time to come and listen to me sing. The songs might also make some fans develop a type of emotional affection for the song's message or even for me as the performer. That's not the same as two people really getting to know each other and feeling love for each other."

"I guess that makes sense. It explains why Elvis Presley, The Beatles and that Sinatra guy were so popular with women. But from what I read, many of them had affairs because of that tempting adoration. Can you really resist that?"

"That I can promise because I have resisted. While I might love the attention my fans give me, I know it's the oxytocin not me."

"Stop being modest. I know for a fact there's at least a little of you in that mix."

"Okay, if you say so. And if it's really my charm that's working on you, then come with me and I'll buy you a glass of Ventura wine. My mom and grandfather will be very happy. After me and your parents, they are your biggest fans. One more thing, my career, unlike your ex's cover story, requires me to travel a great deal. If you weren't working, I could take you and Michele with me, but I would never ask you to give up your career. Can you work with that?"

"I think so. We have lots of holidays and time between classes. We'll be off from Christmas Eve until January fourth, for example, and at other holidays, like Easter, we have some days off, and in the summer from early June to late August."

"Not a bad beginning. There's also Zoom, cell phones and I heard they even have these flying machines, which can quickly transport people from place to place."

"I heard about those. I remember how excited you were when you showed me those wings the nice lady gave you when you came to visit. I'm sure Michele would get into that. Did you know that I spent a year after graduation in Canada to immerse myself in English? When I flew there and back, no one gave me wings."

Michael smiled with a twinkle in his eye. "I'll tell you what. I still have the two wings in my house in Connecticut. I'll give one to you and one to Michele. You both can start a mother-son collection."

Sophia smiled. "Thank you. We'd love that."

As they held hands during that special moment, an irritated voice came from the Mariano vineyard side of the gate.

"Sophia! Is that person bothering you?"

Startled, Sophia turned to see Lorenzo, her former husband, a handsome, well-dressed man staring at Michael, apparently annoyed at seeing them being so intimate.

"Lorenzo! What are you doing here? You said you couldn't come to see Michele until Christmas."

Lorenzo crossed into the Ventura property to confront Michael. "Never mind that. Who are you?"

Michael extended his hand. "It's nice to finally meet you. I'm Michael. My grandfather owns this vineyard. I am an old friend of Sophia's and we've been working on one of her school projects."

Lorenzo moved aggressively into Michael's space in a confronting manner. "I don't like anyone taking liberties with my Sophia."

"First of all, Lorenzo, she is not your Sophia anymore, and secondly, I have the highest respect for her and resent your intimation."

Lorenzo angrily moved to push Michael to the ground.

Michael reacted very swiftly, stepping aside and tossing

Lorenzo, who landed hard. Michael then reached out to help him up.

"Lorenzo, I'm not looking for trouble. Why don't you go and spend some quality time with your son? He is a wonderful young man and needs to see he has a father who cares. Please go now. Sophia will be there after our meeting."

Lorenzo thought briefly about having another confrontation with Michael, who stared at him in an intimidating way. Lorenzo grumbled under his breath as he left.

"Non finisce qui."

Sophia took Michael's hand. "Michael I'm sorry about that. Lorenzo can be a bit of a hothead."

"I'd never have guessed. By the way, what did he say as he took off?"

"He said this isn't over."

Michael became more serious. "I thought it might be something like that. Should I be concerned and ask my security people to deal with him?"

Sophia gave Michael a hug. "You bruised his ego more than his backside. Lorenzo is a lover, not a fighter. He was just trying to save face. Knowing him, he'll be gone after he sees Michele and then hook up with some woman that he can impress by buying her things."

Michael took Sophia into his embrace lovingly. "I really want to be there for Michele to help make up for this guy who is more like a stranger who visits occasionally instead of being a dad who cares."

"Michele would like that, and I would like you two to really get to know each other. Now I better get home and make sure Lorenzo does right by his son before he disappears again."

Michael turned to leave but then stopped and turned.

"After Lorenzo leaves, I'm going to take you and Michele on a special outing. Let me know when you and he have the time and I'll make arrangements."

Chapter 19

ROLLER COASTER AHEAD

Sophia blew a kiss and rushed off. Michael straightened his shoulders and walked bristly through the rows of vines and started to whistle. As Sophia approached the Mariano's parking area, Lorenzo's driver, Enzo, was standing next to his black Mercedes, smoking a cigarette. Because he was a vulgar, brutish man who said insulting things to her in the past, she tried to avoid him whenever she could. When he turned to look toward the vineyards, she quickly walked to the front door.

"Scappi da Enzo? Perché' Ehi maestra che fai non vieni a casa mia e m'insegni a fare l'amore." (Hey teacher, why you run from Enzo? You should come to my house and let me teach you how to make love.)

Sophia ignored him and quickly entered. Lorenzo came out of the living room in an angry mood.

"You've been teaching Michele to hate his father. Now I have to bring him presents on Christmas to bribe him, my own son."

"Why don't you just show him you love him by seeing him more often?"

"Your mother told me who your fancy man is. You shouldn't trust him. He probably has more women than I do."

"Michael entertains them. You just use them. Go and take your vulgar driver who wants to have sex with me."

"Enzo is always joking. You have no sense of humor, that's why we broke up."

"Oh. Is that why? I guess keeping those three women in apartments for your lust was your act of kindness and I didn't understand your good deeds."

"Ah, there's no talking to you."

Lorenzo left, slamming the door behind him. He signaled Enzo to get in and drive. As Enzo started to drive out of the property, Lorenzo tapped him on his shoulder.

"Cosa hai detto a Sophia?" (What did you say to Sophia?)

"Niente di che...le ho fatto i complimenti perche'fa l'insegnante." (Not much...I complimented her on being a teacher.)

"Conosco i tuoi complimenti...non le rivolgerle mai più la parola...ho già abbastanza guai...lei mi ha fatto odiare da mio figlio e sta con questo fichetto...sua madre mi ha detto che è uno famoso. Mentre non stavo guardando mi ha spinto e mi sono fatto male alla schiena." (I know your compliments... don't talk to her again...I have enough trouble...she made my kid hate me and has this fancy boyfriend. Her mother told me he's a big celebrity. When I wasn't looking, he pushed me, and I hurt my back.)

"Vuole che me la veda io con questo?" (Want me to take care of him for you?)

"Queste celebrità hanno le guardie del corpo, meglio che non fai niente... La madre di Sophia ha detto che sta da suo nonno nel vigneto qui accanto...questi vecchi contadini hanno le pistole." (These celebrities have bodyguards, you better not. He's staying with his grandfather on the next vineyard...these old farmers have guns.)

Enzo kept his eyes on the road but was thinking of how he could help Lorenzo with this celebrity creep. He was sure Sophia complained about him and Lorenzo not only paid him well, he set him up with lots of ragazze. They drove late into the night and finally arrived at Lorenzo's northern home near Venice.

The next day Michael was energized, working in the field with several of the grape pickers. Pietro walked over and noticed how much Michael had changed since he came to help his grandfather.

"You are a much different person than when you first came. I see it in your face, the way you walk, and I can hear it in your voice. Is it us or is it a woman?"

Michael stopped working momentarily and took a deep breath. "I guess both have had an influence. Of course, this place, its people, working in the fresh air all helped my spirit. l also found my old friend who I'm very fond of."

Pietro nodded. "Sophia is a wonderful person and a beautiful woman. You are a lucky man."

Michael looked at Pietro questioningly. "How do you know about Sophia?"

Pietro smiled broadly. "I knew that time by the gate that day Sophia felt she had to sneak off. I'm Italian. We know amore when we see it or even hear it."

"So, you have an Italian cupid thing going for you?"

"Could be, but Aurelio also told me this morning. He is so happy he'll probably tell everyone he sees."

"Great... I better tell my manager before it gets out on social media and the wire services. One more thing. Can we wrap up this part of the work shortly? If you don't need me, I'm going to work on the fundraising for the high school."

Pietro was now in a playful mood. "I think one of our neighbors is also working on that project. Maybe you should get together with her."

Michael playfully punched Pietro's shoulder. "Wiseass! You've been talking to my mother."

"I'm officially letting you go. You don't have to pick grapes if I'm invited to the wedding."

Before Michael could react, Pietro waved goodbye.

Michael finished off the work in the vineyard and felt good about being able to concentrate on the school project with Sophia, getting back to his career and having more free time to relax. The next day Sophia called.

"If you're still up for it, Saturday would be a good time to take the trip with Michele."

"Great. I'll set it up."

"By the way, Lorenzo was freaked out when Michele actually said to him 'I don't talk to strangers.' He promised Michele he would come for Christmas and do something special. There is one other thing I wanted to warn you about. Lorenzo is a bit of a coward, but his driver who also doubles as his bodyguard is a guy named Enzo. He is a tough, mean-spirited guy from my experience. With him around, I'm not so sure Lorenzo's anger is not a concern."

"I hope Lorenzo does follow up to do the right thing for his son. A father is very important to a young boy. I can vouch for that. On the threat, if this guy Enzo becomes an issue, I will deal with him, or I'll have one of my security guys take care of it. Please don't worry about it."

Michael went to the desk and took out a sheet with a telephone number, then made a call before getting back to Sophia.

"I'll pick you two up on Saturday at seven."

"Where are we going?"

Michael whispered into the phone. "It will be a surprise."

Sophia thought for a moment. "Okay...but you know I'm not big on surprises."

Michael scratched his head for a moment. "You're a teacher. Think of it as a learning experience."

He hung up quickly and went to his laptop to download the information for Cavalino Mato, an amusement park. The directions estimated it to be an hour-and-forty-two-minute drive from Sophia's. Michael still had the website on his laptop when Manuela came in the office and noticed he was smiling.

"What is making my son smile today?"

Michael leaned back his hands behind his head. "I'm taking Sophia and Michele on Saturday to an amusement park. I'm just looking at the fun rides and hoping they bring some happy memories for the boy."

Manuela came around the desk to look at the pictures. "It does look like fun. I'm happy you are taking an interest in that child. He needs a male role model."

Michael cleared his throat. "Not sure I qualify as a role model for a ten-year-old."

Manuela tapped his shoulder. "Don't sell yourself short. That family needs you. How about I pack you a picnic lunch to make it special?"

"Sound likes a great idea. But nothing with garlic."

Manuela laughed and nodded that she understood his meaning.

The trip to the amusement park was a great success. Going on the different rides with Michael and his Mom made Michele feel special. During the visit, Michael was recognized by fans and had to ask them to give him some space pointing to Michele. Fortunately, they understood and allowed the three to enjoy the day. Michele gave Michael a big hug when they returned home and promised to teach Michael better soccer skills. Sophia was so happy that Michele had a special day, she gave Michael a long goodbye kiss.

"Thank you so much. It was a special day, and I do like this type of surprise."

Michael kissed her back. "I hope we can share more special days long after our business here is over. That reminds me, don't we have a final meeting scheduled this week?"

"We sure do. I think we better start preparing tonight."

Michael and Sophia met in Aurelio's office to finalize everything for the concert and checklist that ticket sales had filled the Teatro dei Renovate in Siena and all the talent had confirmed. They made sure the social media fundraising site was working and found it was already receiving donations. Because Michael and several well-known singers had agreed to perform, the event would be televised as well as streamed through the internet. When they were finished, Michael looked over to Sophia.

"What do you think about my asking Emma to do a duet at the event? Since this fundraiser is to benefit the students, they should be represented."

"That's a wonderful idea. That would also be a boost to our school's music program, which is always under scrutiny when the budget is tight."

Michael became excited. "Then that's what we'll do. Last night I spoke to Billy, who assured me the technical part is all set, and Gerry arranged for an experienced stage manager who'll be there to make sure the event has none of those nasty glitches."

Sophia hugged Michael enthusiastically. "Thank you for making this happen. I don't think any of us realized what it takes to put on this type of concert. We are used to school productions and music recitals in our own auditorium."

"Hey, I was glad I could help. It made me realize how much I enjoy the action. I hope your committee members weren't upset because we took over the final preparations."

"I think they were relieved. They have their family obligations and other school duties."

"What about Matteo? Is everything okay?"

Sophia nodded. "Yes! We had the talk. When I suggested he take Anna out and he did it so quickly, I think I was insulted...just kidding. I was happy they hit it off. Although I had a feeling there were some sparks between them already."

Michael looked pleased. "That is good news. Now, how should we celebrate?"

Sophia put up her hands. "Maybe we should wait until after the concert."

"You're probably right. We have an old expression. Don't count your chickens before they hatch."

Sophia pointed with her finger. "We have our own expression, mai promettere sole prima che sorga."

"Why does that sound more exotic when you say it?"

"When you become bilingual, you will find out. Before I forget to ask, can we leave for Tina's wedding at seven thirty? The wedding is at ten and it's almost a two-hour drive to Lucca if we don't run into construction or accident delays. I am bringing something for Tina's mom from my mother, so I wanted to make sure we aren't late. Is that okay?"

"I'll be up and ready to go. I also wanted to get over to the reception place to make sure my DJ guy is set up and ready to welcome them to the reception properly. Come on, I'll walk you home."

By the time Michael came back to the farmhouse, he found Aurelio still up and waiting for him. He ushered Michael into the office.

"Michael, I have some sad news. My old friend Gerhard Schmidt died. I received a call from his oldest son, Max, who said that his dad put in his will that if no one in his family wanted to use the property in Italy to offer it to me as his favorite neighbor, or to someone in our family. He said the six-bedroom villa, all seventy hectares of land that includes the vineyards and a small lake. He put a price of two point seven million euros. I said that was very nice of Gerhard. I will ask my family. The only one I know who could afford to buy it is you. Before I say no thank you, I wanted to talk to you."

"I remember visiting him when we were kids, and I loved that house. So did Sophia. I have three questions. Is that a decent deal pricewise? How many acres is 70 hectares? And are the vineyard's grapes any good for expanding your operation?"

Aurelio thought for a moment. "I asked my real estate friend before you came. He said that price would be below market by twenty to twenty-five percent and that seventy hectares is like your one hundred and seventy acres. Yes, I believe with some work, their vineyards could add another thirty percent to our wine production in two or three years."

"Let me make a call to my financial guy."

Michael suddenly became energized and went to his room and made the call. Michael learned there was no problem with cash flow. Michael could sign a contract anytime he wanted and have the money wired from his bank. Within two weeks, he would have the balance from two tax-free municipal funds coming due and the option of selling a few stocks if he wanted to close before the end of the fiscal year.

Michael went down to see Aurelio.

"Let's take a quick trip over to see the house. If it's in reasonable condition, you can call their son, make the deal. Tell the son to have Gerhard's attorney who handles the estate to call my attorney."

Michael handed Aurelio the attorney's contact information.

Michael then called the caretaker and went with Manuela and Aurelio over to Gerhard's property. The caretaker showed them through the house, which was in very good condition, then they all went look at the vineyards and lake. Manuela was impressed with everything about it.

"I hope you invite your favorite mother to stay here

sometime. It's an amazing place. My dad is really excited and looking forward to developing the vineyards. If you need a contractor to make any changes, I know someone who does great work in this area."

Chapter 20

THE WEDDING IN LUCCA

On the day of Tina's wedding, Michael and Sophia arrived in front of a church in Lucca. Michael got out of the car to look at the architecture and helped Sophia unload a large package.

"It looks like that church has been around a long time."

Sophia nodded.

"This one is the Basilica of San Frediano. It is the oldest church in the city. It was built I believe in the 12th century."

Michael looked impressed.

"Then it's a thousand years old...and I have my own beautiful tour guide who knows these things. You go in and make your cousin Tina's mom happy and I'll go to the reception hall and check on my DJ. By the way, you do look amazing."

Sophia blushed and waved a "stop it, you're embarrassing me" gesture. She then stopped momentarily to look at Michael and came back to kiss him on the cheek.

"Thank you for doing this, and the compliment is also appreciated."

Michael was smiling to himself as he drove slowly down the street looking for the hotel, which turned out to be modest from the outside but charming on the inside. The DJ was already in the reception room setting up his equipment. When Michael came in, he stopped what he was doing to greet Michael effusively and thanked him for arranging the gig. As Michael set up the microphone that the DJ brought for him, he checked out the layout of the room by walking around. He looked at the cards with the guests' names until he found Sophia's and un amico.

Michael was standing behind a partition when the wedding guests entered and found their way to their assigned tables. The DJ was set up with his equipment at the back of the small stage. He played a recording of TUA by Nilla Pizzi, which was a favorite welcoming melody at weddings. The professional-looking microphone was in front with an impressive-looking sound system off to the side near the partition. Because everyone expected a simple DVD player, the guests became curious about the sophisticated setup. This caused lots of animated conversation at the tables. Sophia and her family were seated at the table nearest the left side of the stage. She looked around the room, curious about where Michael was hiding. When the bride and groom entered, the DJ switched the music to a more rousing Tarantella and the guests started clapping to the beat. Tina responded to the clapping with a few of her own exuberant dance steps, making everyone laugh and cheer. Her new husband, Tommaso, who was an accountant, just wondered about all the fuss.

As the music welcoming the bride and groom ended, Michael came quickly out from behind the partition and jumped up on the small stage and took the microphone off the stand.

"Hi, everyone! My name is Michael, and I was invited to sing one of Tina's favorite American love songs for her and

Tommaso."

Tina and some of the younger family members immediately recognized Michael and she began to jump up and
down and the others began to clap and cheer as Michael began
singing. Everyone quieted down as he performed "When I Fall
in Love," written by Victor Young and Edward Heyman, which
became a staple for many singers over the years. It was
popular in Italy because it had a resurgence when featured in
Sleepless in Seattle, an iconic American romantic comedy.

Tina excitedly looked over at Sophia and pointed to him
then her and mouthed, "Is he yours?"

Sophia nodded.

Tina grinned widely and gave a thumbs up to show her
approval.

When Michael finished, Tina pulled Tommaso by his hand
up to Michael, who came off the platform to meet them. Tina
gave Michael a big kiss on both cheeks and a big embrace,
whispering something in his ear. Michael nodded and while
the wedding couple stood in front of him, he went back up on
the small stage and consulted with the DJ, who nodded and
started the music playing.

Michael came down and took Tina and Tommaso and had
them hold hands and look at each other.

Michael sang to the couple one of his signature old
standards, "The Way You Look Tonight."

It was a song which he had already planned to sing at his
Christmas concert.

As he sang to the newlyweds, he also kept glancing
occasionally over at Sophia making her blush. Many of the
guests turned to see to whom his gaze was going and were
thrilled when they saw Sophia blushing. Maria, who was
sitting across from her daughter, noticed, and smiled then
elbowed Francesco who was clueless about what was going
on.

When Michael finished the song, he came off the stage to warmly greet everyone who rushed forward. Sophia had tears in her eyes seeing how happy everyone was that she brought her famous friend to Tina's wedding. Michael gave a signal to the DJ to play dance music then went to Sophia and took her hand and they danced to slow dance music very, very close.

Sophia went cheek to cheek, pressed against Michael, then she whispered in a sexy voice, "Do you think my father will bring a ruler while we dance?"

Michael laughed quietly and nuzzled her neck, whispering in her ear. "Let's not go there. Remember, he bought a second horse when we were children, so we didn't even ride together."

Sophia suddenly felt a tap on her shoulder and turned to see Tina with her bouquet in one hand and her garter in the other.

"Hai reso questo giorno molto speciale... Voglio che voi due abbiate questi. E voglio che Michael balli con me." (You made this day very special... I want you two to have these. And I want Michael to dance with me.)

Sophia took the bouquet and gave her cousin a kiss on the cheek and a big hug.

"Hai reso questo giorno molto speciale... Voglio che voi due abbiate questi. E voglio che Michael balli con me." (Be my guest but give him back...he has to drive me home.)

As Tina boldly took Michael in hand to dance with her, the guests started clapping and some of the men whistled. Sophia saw that Tommaso felt a little intimidated by having a celebrity dancing with his new wife. She smiled at him and gestured for him to dance with her. He became animated and walked over quickly, which made the guests whistle and clap again.

After the dance with Tina, Michael and Sophia sat down to eat with the rest of the guests. Maria nodded at Michael with the biggest smile he had ever seen on Sophia's mother.

"Michael, you were very generous to make Tina's wedding so special. The family thanks you for your kindness and hopes you will think of us as your family. My brother Vito is one of the finest bakers in all of Tuscany and Tina's father. He told me to tell you that when you get married, he will personally make you a magnificent wedding cake."

Michael was speechless, not knowing how to react to the unusual offer from the father of the bride. Sophia, who was surprised by such a personal offer, misunderstood Michael's reaction.

"Mamma. That is a very generous offer from Uncle Vito. Please tell him that Michael will contact Vito if and when he does."

Maria, though disappointed, nodded. "I will tell Vito."

As they were leaving the wedding, Michael sought out Tommaso to thank him for the invitation and handed him an envelope that contained a beautiful card and a check for a thousand Euros. On the way out, Sophia reached over to grip Michael's elbow.

"Everybody was so excited that you made this night one to remember. I hope you weren't put off by my Uncle Vito's offer."

Michael turned to Sophia. "You kidding? That was the most awesome gift offer I have ever received. Uncle Vito's offer is not only from the heart. Baking is his craft, and a wedding cake is his art and to offer me his best creation would be like having a master painter offer to do the wedding portrait. I think that's what left me speechless. Thank you for having my back because I really didn't know what to say."

As they reached the street in front of the hotel, Sophia stopped Michael and took both his hands and made intense eye contact.

"While you were talking to Tommaso, Tina asked me if I

would stay for a family breakfast. Her dad surprised her during the second father-daughter dance. Apparently, Uncle Vito planned it without her or his wife knowing. He's always been such a solitary hard-working man who never does things like that. Tina made a reservation for me at the bed and breakfast down the street because the hotel rooms here were all booked. What do you think?"

"Of course, you should go. Family is very important. But how will you get home in the morning?"

Sophia let go of Michael's hands and gripped his shoulders tightly and pulled him very close. "There are two possibilities. You could leave now, and I can go back with my parents, or you could stay with me tonight, go the breakfast in the morning and drive me home as planned."

Michael cleared his throat. "Are you sure? I'm really not that good of a driver."

"Please don't joke, Michael. I'm being serious. Inviting you to be with me overnight is a little outside my comfort zone."

Michael put his arms around Sophia and pulled her into him and kissed her then smiled. "Then I choose possibility number two, because the truth is, I do prefer to drive in the daylight, and I feel a little sweaty and could use a hot shower right now with my beautiful passenger."

Sophia laughed despite herself and punched his arm lovingly and hugged him back. "Then let's check out the bathing facilities."

As soon as they entered their quaintly decorated room in the charming B&B, Michael took Sophia into his arms and kissed her passionately on her neck, face, and lips. She responded by taking off his jacket, then his tie, and even unbuttoning his shirt and tossing them all on a nearby chair. He reciprocated by taking down the zipper on the back of her dress. Before they knew it, he was in his shorts, and she was down to her bra and panties. Without saying another word,

Sophia took Michael by the hand into the bathroom and turned on the shower as they finished undressing. After she put her hand to test that the water was hot enough, she pulled Michael into it.

That night all their childhood disappointments, teenage embarrassments, current misunderstandings, frustrations, and unspoken desires were washed away in an intense round of sensual pleasuring, which lasted for hours and ended with them asleep in each other's arms.

When they awoke, Sophia felt Michael's head on her bare back and looked down at his arm around her waist. She snuggled against him then suddenly her eyes opened wide, and she picked up her cellphone to look at the time. Sophia sat up immediately and pushed Michael's shoulder until he was awake.

"Michael, we have only 25 minutes to get to the breakfast. Remember, you are also invited."

"You sure you want your parents to know I stayed?"

"In case you haven't noticed, I'm not a little girl anymore. I have no problem with that."

"Actually, I did notice you weren't a little girl anymore the first day I visited your school. Last night confirmed what a stunning woman you've become. Of course, I'd love to have breakfast with your family."

When Michael and Sophia approached the hotel dining room entrance, there were sounds of loud conversations going on in Italian. As they entered, the room went silent. Large round tables were set up with eight seats at each. At the table where Tina and Tommaso sat with their parents, there were two empty seats. Tina stood up to indicate that Michael and Sophia should sit with them. Somewhat embarrassed that their arrival stopped everyone's conversation, Sophia looked at Tina to explain the reaction of the quests. She understood and came over to welcome the new arrivals.

"Nessuno tranne me sapeva che potevi essere qui nem- meno i tuoi genitori, quindi il tuo ingresso è stato uno spettacolo." (No one but me knew that you might be here, not even your parents, so your entrance was a showstopper).

Sophia made a gesture with her hands, indicating she felt badly because everyone stopped what they were doing.

"Ho detto a Michael che saremmo potuti entrare alla chetichella come gli altri di famiglia." (I told Michael we could slip in quietly and just be one of the families.)

Tina smiled and waved a "you are kidding" gesture to her cousin.

"Dopo l'apparizione a sorpresa di Michael ieri sera, entrare inosservato non è neanche un'opzione." (After Michael's sur- prise appearance last night, slipping in unnoticed is not an option.)

While Sophia explained what was going on to Michael, everyone stood up at the tables and began clapping, including the parents of the bride and groom.

Michael whispered to Sophia with a coy smile on his face, "So much for slipping in, but I guess having some new fans in beautiful Lucca is worth a little awkward moment or two."

Sophia turned and addressed the family members.

"Michele vi ringrazia tutti per la generosa accoglienza ma vuole che tutti si divertano e festeggino il matrimonio di Tina e Tommaso mangiando a quattro ganasce a questa festa organizzata dal suo amorevole papà." (Michael thanks you all for your generous reception. He wants everyone to enjoy themselves and celebrate Tina and Tommaso's marriage by eating heartily at this feast arranged by her loving father.)

With that said, everyone sat down as the waiters served the food and Sophia and Michael sat with Tina, who beamed with pride having Michael sitting next to her. Sophia kept busy translating from Italian to English and English to Italian.

While Michael understood some of the conversations, the

people at the table spoke too fast for him to translate himself. He did a great deal of nodding and waiting for translations from Sophia during the meal and kept smiling his appreciation and accepting nods and smiles in return.

As they drove home after the breakfast, Sophia looked over at Michael, who was focused on driving.

"Michael, I don't want to embarrass you, but you were a lovemaking virtuoso last night. You had to be taught by a loving woman how to pleasure a woman because it was a night this woman will never forget."

Michael suddenly remembered Vanessa's teenage tutoring. "It was you who inspired me."

"I'll take the compliment, but truthfully I've never felt anything like you made me feel."

"Making me think about last night with you is making this driver very distracted to maneuver these windy roads. Can we talk about it the next time we can reprise that amazing night?"

"That sounds like a good plan. As a teacher, I absolutely approve of repeating a lesson plan that engages the student."

Sophia then smiled at the thought, rubbed Michael's arm lovingly and closed her eyes and fell asleep. Michael was replaying the morning in his head as he drove, remembering how he was touched by the family's warm acceptance and their send off with hugs and kisses. Uncle Vito was especially demonstrative effusively thanking him for making his daughter's wedding an event that she would treasure the memory and tell her grandchildren. Michael shook off his thoughts to concentrate on the road but then glanced over at Sophia and smiled. He gripped the steering wheel and kept his eyes on the road, enjoying the quiet.

After driving for over an hour, Michael remembered he had to get back to his attorney. He thought what better time to check off that box than stopping there on the way home. He made one more call and said only a few words.

"Hi Ben. That property purchase by my grandfather's is a go. Keep me posted on a closing date."

The call caused Sophia to wake up.

"Are we almost there?"

Michael looked over and touched Sophia's arm.

"Now you sound like I did when my dad took us on a long trip. We're still about an hour away. I was thinking, would you be up to stopping at the old lake we used to swim when we were kids?"

"You're serious?"

"Of course. It'll be fun to revisit the place."

"If you're game, I would love to revisit the place. I went there when I didn't hear from you and cried at the place where we used to jump in."

"Well, this time we'll be there together, but no crying, and I'm not jumping in."

Sophia laughed. "I won't either, especially not in this dress."

Chapter 21

THE UNEXPECTED

Earlier that morning, Lorenzo woke up after having a fretful night's sleep. He looked over at the woman sleeping next to him. He pushed her shoulder hard until she was awake and told her she had to leave. When she said that she first had to take a shower, he told her to do it at her own place. When she protested, he reached into his wallet, pulled out three two-hundred-Euro notes and handed them to her. She took them, then cursed at him for treating her like a prostitute but grabbed her clothes and left in a huff.

Lorenzo called the Mariano house to talk to his son. Maria told him that she, Francesco, Sophia and Michael had gone to a family event.

"We just arrived ourselves and expected them shortly. I called my friends who are taking care of Michele, but the housekeeper said they went out to eat somewhere."

Lorenzo suppressed his anger and said he had a present for Michele and wanted to bring it today. Maria said he should wait for Sophia to get back because he wasn't expected until

Christmas. Lorenzo was furious that he had to wait to talk to his ex to see his own child.

He called Enzo to bring the car. When the chauffeur arrived, Lorenzo was still in a rage. He told Enzo he wasn't going to let Sophia, or her new boyfriend take his son away from him. He's decided to bring his Christmas present early. It was an expensive Xbox Series X console and that would make Michele happy.

As Michael drove, Sophia was reminiscing about their happy times at the lake. She remembered the day Mr. Schmidt came and invited them to see his gardens and later how Aurelio brought them to visit the villa. Michael picked up on it quickly

"That's a good idea. Let's go by his old house while we're there."

Michael drove into the property, observing the beauty of the tree-lined gravel driveway as they approached the grand villa. He parked the car and quickly escorted Sophia on the path to the lake and only stopped when they were at their favorite entrance point.

"You certainly have a good memory. I don't think I would have remembered how to get here from the main road."

"I guess the place made an impression on me."

Sophia took Michael's hand and squeezed it. "We probably should leave before we get in trouble."

"Aurelio knows the caretaker. I asked him to let the guy know in case we decided to drop by. Come, let's go look at the house."

Sophia looked at Michael questioningly. "You are full of surprises."

Sophia noticed when Michael rang the bell how quickly the caretaker invited them to go through the beautifully restored villa. As they went through the rooms, Sophia became starry-eyed at all the interior design elegance and exquisite architectural detailing.

"This place is even more beautiful than I remembered."

"It is nice, isn't it? Be great to have a house like this, wouldn't it?"

"What is that American expression? It would be like winning the lottery."

Michael laughed. "That would depend on how much you win taking it upfront and after taxes. I should get you home."

As they started to leave, the caretaker asked if Michael would talk to him privately. Michael asked Sophia to wait in the car for a minute. The caretaker knew about the possible sale and wondered what Michael thought about the house place and intended to do about him.

"Everything looks great. I'm going to need you so please stay on. I have a concert in Rome and a tour next year to deal with. I'll ask Aurelio to coordinate while I'm away. Right now, we have to go."

Michael quickly slid into the driver's seat to leave. Sophia tapped his shoulder. "What was that all about?"

"He asked me what I thought about how he took care of the house. I said everything looked terrific."

When Lorenzo arrived at the Mariano farmhouse, Sophia and Michael weren't back from their visit to the Schmidt estate and Michele had not arrived from his friend's home. Lorenzo started yelling at Maria for allowing his son to stay with her friend's family. Francesco heard the commotion and grabbed him roughly by the arm and told him to wait outside or he would throw him out.

Lorenzo sat in the car with Enzo. He was fuming that he came all the way here and Michele wasn't back yet. He blamed Michael for turning everyone against him. When Michael's car finally arrived and stopped by the front of the farmhouse to let Sophia out, Enzo watched as Lorenzo clutched his fists. Lorenzo waited for Michael to drive away before getting out of the car and telling Enzo he would be a while. He was going to settle his right to see his son once and for all.

After dropping Sophia off at the Mariano farmhouse, Michael immediately called Ben at his home.

"Ben, it's Michael again. I want to close the Schmidt deal right after the Christmas concert."

When Michael pulled up to the house, he noticed there was a new pickup truck with a construction company sign printed on the side. Curious what the truck was doing there, Michael hurried inside and went toward Aurelio's office, thinking there was a business meeting. When he heard people talking in the kitchen, he quickly turned back and went there. Michael was surprised to find his mother sitting next to a big, rugged, good-looking man.

Back at the Mariano vineyard, Enzo watched as his boss knocked politely and then entered the farmhouse. He had already decided to take care of the bastardo neighbor to prove his loyalty to Lorenzo. He waited five minutes until he was sure Lorenzo wouldn't get thrown out again. Enzo quietly got out of the car and took the tire iron from the trunk. He went through the connecting gate through the Ventura vineyards until he could see the house where he heard the stronzo ragazzo was staying. The BMW was also out front, so Enzo knew his prey was inside.

Manuela was surprised and elated to see Michael standing at the kitchen threshold.

"Michael, I'm so happy you came home in time. I want you to meet Alessandro. He's an old friend from my high school days."

Alessandro stood up. He was dressed in a neat but casual fashionable style that could be found in a LL Bean Catalogue. He was also an impressive, good-looking man who towered over everyone. He quickly came over and extended his hand to Michael.

"Nice to finally meet you, Michael. Manuela has been bragging about you for years."

"Nice meeting you, Alessandro. I do remember mom talking about visiting her high school friends, but you are a surprise."

Manuela came over and took Michael's arm then turned to Aurelio and Alexandro. "I have to go over something important with Michael. Be right back."

She pulled Michael into Aurelio's office and closed the door.

"Alessandro has become very special in my life, and I want you to treat him like family."

"When you said you were going into town to see your high school friends, I always assumed it was female classmates. Don't get me wrong, Alessandro seems like a nice guy. I presume that's his truck and he's a building contractor near-by."

"Actually, he has a very big construction business. He does both residential and commercial work all over Tuscany and in Milan and Venice."

"That's impressive. Sorry if my reaction made him or you feel uncomfortable. I'm completely on board that you have a special friend, but I did see some of grandfather's goodies on the table and I'm a little hungry."

Manuela laughed. "You always had a good appetite. Come! I want you and Alessandro to be great friends."

As Enzo crept up to the front door with the tire iron in hand, he was so focused on the front door, he tripped on one of the steps and the weapon clanked as he fell onto the porch. He cursed as his right knee hit the pointy edge of the step, which caused a sharp pain to radiate up his leg. He pushed himself up to stand with his left hand and held the tire iron with his right. Enzo was almost upright when the door opened.

Michael stared down at the intruder. Next to him were Alessandro and Manuela. Michael pointed at the tire iron.

"Who are you? Why are you carrying that?"

"Uh...ehm...sono Enzo...pensavo fosse la fattoria dei Mariano. Il mio capo Lorenzo aveva bisogno di una chiave inglese" (Ugh...err...I am Enzo...I thought this was the Mariano farmhouse. My boss, Lorenzo, needed a tire iron.)

Manuela took her cellphone and called Sophia.

"Hi Sophia, there's a man named Enzo carrying a tire iron at our front door. He said it is for Lorenzo."

"Enzo is Lorenzo's driver and bodyguard. He was parked outside when he brought Lorenzo to visit Michele. Don't know why he would bring a tire iron to your house. Wait... the car is still here so he had to walk through the vineyard to you. I'm sure the jerk is up to no good."

Manuela took out her phone.

"Chiamo la polizia." (I will call the police.)

As soon as Enzo heard the word police, he stood up and tried to grab Manuela's phone while brandishing the tire iron threateningly. Alessandro moved swiftly, grabbed Enzo's arm and twisted it until Enzo dropped the weapon and then put him on the ground and kneeled on his chest. He turned to Manuela.

"Now you should call them."

While they waited, Alessandro restrained the raging chauffeur.

Michael whispered to Manuela. "By the way, I do like the way your high school friend handled himself."

The police came and took Enzo with them. When they charged him and processed his fingerprints, they found several outstanding charges for criminally violent acts in the national database.

When Lorenzo heard what happened, he left the Mariano property quickly and drove off. The next time he called to talk to his son Michele, he called from Spain. He had his well-connected lawyers take care of things when Enzo told the polizia that he was only protecting his boss.

Chapter 22

CONCERT TIME IN SIENA

During the weeks leading up to the concert, Michael and Sophia spent a great deal of time together. While during much of the time they were ironing out details, meeting with committee members, they were becoming a serious couple and their friends and family were rooting for them.

The next week everything began to fall into place. The concert was only a few days away and final plans were coming to fruition. Michael and Sophia met with Billy on the final checklist meeting to make sure the technical aspects were covered. After Billy assured them again that the equipment and the stage people were ready, he put his arms around them.

"Hey, remember you two that I love to go to weddings. Don't forget me."

Being so direct seemed to embarrass Michael and make Sophia feel awkward. After Sophia was out of the room, Michael took his friend's arm and pulled Billy up close.

"My friend, please don't push this marriage talk prematurely. I'm still dealing with some old stuff."

"You mean Louisa."

Michael nodded.

"Look. I'm sorry if I embarrassed you, but I think you two are perfect for each other."

"I can't disagree with you on that, but it's a little complicated."

Billy took Michael's arm.

"Since you've been here, you are a new person from a few months ago. I'm your friend and want you to be happy."

When Gerry heard from Billy what Michael said, he drove up from Rome. Michael greeted Gerry warmly and thanked him for being patient with him. After visiting with Manuela and Aurelio, Michael was excited to show his manager the silver BMW. Gerry pointed to his small Fiat and asked Michael if he would like to swap cars. Michael said he would when Hell froze over. They both had a good laugh and walked over to the Mariano's to have Gerry meet Sophia. After a pleasant two hours just talking and sharing a glass of Mariano vintage, they returned to the Ventura farmhouse.

When they sat down to discuss the Rome concert in Aurelio's office, Gerry looked at Michael and reached out and tapped his hand.

"Did you happen to bring Louisa's letter with you?"

"Of course. It was the last thing I have of hers. Why'd you ask?"

"Because when Louisa handed it to me, that sweet dying woman was more concerned for you than what was happening to her. She made me promise to remind you to live a life of joy, not sorrow or regret. Look, I'm not very good at giving advice about relationships. One thing you learn as you get older is that life is not like a film drama that depends on unresolved conflict to drive the story to the final scene. In real life, if we don't learn to manage disappointments and even tragedies, they will destroy us. In the end, you are the only one who can change your life, and after meeting Sophia, I think you got lucky."

Michael teared up. "I know you're right. It's just hard to forget what Louisa went through. I'm getting there because of good friends like you who care so much. I do care deeply for Sophia, and I believe fate brought her back into my life for a reason. My dear, generous Louisa wrote that letter so I could move on with my life."

Gerry squeezed Michael's wrist as a friendly gesture. "Then I will leave you and your wonderful family and go back to Rome and make my magic. By the way, we'll have to go right after that school fundraiser to get everything ready to help them plan the Christmas concert and arrange next year's tour."

On the day of the fundraiser concert in Siena, Michael arrived to the cheers of his fans who were waiting to greet him. Some were anxious to get his autograph and others to touch him as he passed into the stage door entrance. Sophia acted as his assistant and ushered him through the crowds and into the waiting arms of the Preside.

"Michael and Sophia, I am so happy to see you. As you probably know already, the concert is sold out. The ticket sales and donations we received from the media promotions have put us over our financial goal. I also received a call from your friend, Jim Litman. He said he would personally fund our music and arts programs since we don't need more money for the science and technical improvements."

Michael nodded his head and smiled with satisfaction.

"Jim is an enigma. Though he became a successful engineer, inventor and software development guy through his hard work and perseverance, he loves all the arts. His mom was a professional classical pianist, and he loves to play jazz on his old piano. He really believes that the arts are more important to our daily lives than the things he makes lots of money doing."

The Preside shook Michael's hand. "I understand Mr. Litman is in the audience, so I will acknowledge his generous gift before the concert. And you dear Sophia—everyone in the school is grateful for your successful efforts and for bringing your famous friend to help. I thank both of you on behalf of all the teachers, staff and students for making all this happen."

He reached around both Sophia and Michael and gave them a big bear hug.

"I'm so happy. I now look forward to hearing all this great talent and our wonderful Emma and you. Ciao!"

As the Preside scurried off, Michael and Sophia were still in shock about his uncharacteristic over-the-top enthusiasm. As Michael and Sophia tuned to go into the backstage area, Manuela was waiting with Alessandro.

"We wanted to wish you both much success tonight. I also wanted Sophia to meet my good friend. This is Alessandro. We went to high school together. He met Michael the night that Enzo creep came to Aurelio's house."

Sophia quickly extended her hand. "Welcome Alessandro. Thank you for protecting tonight's star performer. I hope you enjoy the concert."

"Looking forward to it."

Michael, anxious to get on stage, took his mother by her shoulders and kissed her on both cheeks. "I really have to go now. When I get back after the holidays why don't we all have dinner together?"

Manuela smiled. "We will do that."

As Michael led Sophia backstage, she stopped him.

"This was successful because of your efforts and talents. Now our school's students will be able to compete in the global market. Your visit to your grandfather turned out to be a godsend for many others, especially me."

Michael blushed a bit. "Don't underestimate yourself. You

were the driving force. I came along to help, and you and the school gave me new purpose. I needed you as much as you may have thought you needed me, so I thank you and your school for that. Unfortunately, I was informed by Gerry that I will have to leave right after the concert tonight to go to Rome to rehearse for my performance and help to promote the event."

Sophia was somewhat taken aback. "I had hoped you would be able to stay after to wrap up everything and be with me."

Michael gently took Sophia's hands. "I'm as disappointed as you, because you brought me out of a very dark place and made this Christmas concert in Rome and a comeback tour possible. Gerry told me I've been off the media's radar, which makes it extremely important to ensure that Rome is a big success. It is my springboard to a tour next year as well as being an important fundraiser. The entertainment business can be a minefield for a performer and any hint of being off your game can become a PR nightmare."

Sophia squeezed Michael's hands and let go quickly.

"He's right, of course. You must do what you need to. Michael Ventura is not just ours to keep; he's an important international entertainer with fans all over the world who miss him. Don't worry about anything. I'll wrap up the final details with the other committee members. Now go on stage, do your magic, and make this event one that Siena will remember."

Michael watched from behind the curtain until the final stragglers filled the seats. He gave a hand gesture to raise the curtain signal to the stage manager. He quickly stepped out on stage to greet the audience, who clapped until he raised both hands to have them quiet down. The night's entertainment was well organized and fast-paced. There was a diversity of talent from Italy, Canada, the USA, Spain and South America.

They performed brilliantly and had the audience cheering. Michael and Emma did their duet at the end and the audience gave them a standing ovation. All the performers came to take a final bow and received another standing ovation.

Sophia, the Preside and a beaming music teacher were on their feet cheering along with the audience. Michael thanked everyone for making the fundraiser a success. He then asked Sophia and the committee to come onstage for a bow. The audience stood up again to give them a standing ovation. The committee reacted with smiles. Matteo and Anna held hands up high as they showed their appreciation and Matteo nodded a well done to Michael as they left the stage. Michael waved goodbye to the audience

"Grazie a tutti voi siete stati un pubblico meraviglioso." (Thank you all, you've been a wonderful audience.)

Backstage, Gerry was waiting patiently as Michael was surrounded by well-wishers and fans. Gerry finally went up to Michael.

"That was an amazing thing you did. I loved the duet you did with that young girl. Maybe we should think about having her perform with you sometime. The audience loved it."

"I'm game. Emma has the voice of an angel. You would have to plan it during her summer vacation."

"That's a possibility. I believe we play Milan in July. We should go soon, it's a long drive."

Michael looked around at the crowded backstage. "Just give me a few more minutes to say goodbye to Sophia."

Spotting Manuela, he walked over.

"Have you seen Sophia?"

Manuela shrugged. "I saw her after the concert, looking for her parents. I congratulated her and asked if she was happy with everything. She said it was more than amazing and had to go because her parents and Michele were waiting for her."

Michael sighed. "I disappointed her when told her I had to leave right after the concert. If you see her, please tell her the timing was out of my control."

Manuela nodded her understanding. "I'm sure she knows, but Sophia will need to hear from you to be assured you're not disappearing again."

Michael gave Manuela a hug. "I'll definitely keep in touch from Rome. See you soon."

Michael turned to Gerry, who gave him the "we have to leave" sign, and they quickly exited the backstage door.

During the next week, Michael and Gerry stayed at the Rome Cavalieri and worked long hours helping to organize the Christmas Concert. Between the promotional work meeting with press, social media influencers and with the representatives of the other talents, the two men were exhausted. Gerry said they would take Sunday off to recuperate. Gerry suggested they have dinner at his favorite family restaurant in one of the nearby neighborhoods where Michael wouldn't be recognized.

Chapter 23

ADVENTURES IN ROME

Michael and Gerry were finally relaxed and enjoying a glass of wine while waiting for their dinner in a small neighborhood restaurant. Michael noticed a group of young women at a nearby table celebrating the engagement of one of their friends. He was drawn to their joyful, friendly banter and infectious laughter. Gerry was taken off guard when Michael called the waiter over and told him to put their bill on his tab. The waiter cautioned Michael that the group had been there for two hours and had been drinking and their bill was already over three hundred Euros. Michael said that was okay. The waiter shrugged and said he would bring him their bill.

As the waiter left, he made a gesture to the cashier that his customer was a little crazy. Michael and Gerry continued their conversation about finalizing his preparation to rehearse and plan a final checklist for the other talents. They became so engrossed in the discussion; Michael didn't notice that the women from the engagement celebration were all standing next to him. A tall imposing woman tapped him on the shoulder. When Michael looked up, she pointed to herself.

"Me, Elena...I speak little English...cameriere say you pay for party...why pay?"

Michael spoke slowly and was animated with his personal sign-language, some Italian words and lots of hand gestures.

"I'm happy that you were all allegra con le amiche, I wanted to pay for making me happy too."

The woman showed him her cellphone with his picture promoting the concert. "This you?"

Michael nodded.

"You famoso cantante...why in piccolo ristorante?"

Michael smiled pointed at the food then made a gesture rubbing his stomach, which made the women giggle.

"Buono!"

Elena translated her understanding of what Michael said so her friends could understand then they smiled.

"Grazie! You buono cantante."

Elena then bent down and hugged Michael who quickly stood up and kissed her on both cheeks while one of the other friends took their picture with her cellphone. Each of the women gave him a hug and kissed him on both cheeks. Gerry stood up amused then gestured kiddingly to the women, "what about me?" All the women then came over and hugged him. They all left the restaurant laughing, leaving Michael and Gerry standing as the restaurant exploded with clapping and cheering. Both men took a bow and sat down until their meal arrived. Gerry looked at Michael and grinned.

"I can't take you anywhere without women hugging you, can I?"

Michael shrugged just as the waiter served them their dinner.

When Michael woke up on Sunday, he felt the urge to have a run. He put on his sweats and asked the Portiera (concierge) where there was a good place for a Sunday run and was told to head to the Tiber River paths, which would be less crowded in the early morning. Michael followed his advice and ran past the walkers on the path that wound its way through a variety of interesting areas and beautiful scenery. As he did, he felt his energy returning and began thinking of Sophia and decided to call her later that morning.

After he showered and dressed, he called Gerry, who sounded sleepy, and asked if he wanted breakfast. Gerry said he was going back to sleep and would get room service later. Michael thought that sounded like a good idea and ordered an American breakfast with eggs and pancakes from room service. He turned on his laptop to see the local news and watch a movie online to relax. The lead on the news was a picture of Elena hugging him and the anchor telling the story of his paying their bill. He leaned back and put his hands over his eyes thinking there is no privacy anymore. To clear his head from the rest of the negative news coverage of crime and disasters that followed, he watched a romantic comedy but fell asleep before the ending. When he woke up, it was almost noon. He remembered he wanted to call Sophia. When he opened his phone, he saw a text from Gerry and Michael shook his head in amazement and spurted aloud.

"Unbelievable."

Sophia was just returning from a walk to the gate between the two vineyard properties, when her cell beeped with a new message. It was from Michael, who sent her the link about the media coverage on the story about the girls from the restaurant. As she watched it, Sophia remembered Michael's talk about how he dealt with his celebrity. She thought it was a nice story, which reported his generous payment of the engagement party's tab and ended with the women hugging Michael. Sophia's cellphone rang again. It was Michael.

"Michael, I just saw that story about you and on those women and was just thinking how being a celebrity becomes newsworthy even when you don't want it to be."

"Welcome to my world. Must have been a slow day in the newsroom. Here's the rest of that story. While I napped in my hotel room, I had a text from Gerry that the concert promoter called him to say after social media went viral with it, online ticket sales were through the roof as well as contribution pledges. So that old Hollywood adage that any publicity is good apparently has some validity. Now the promoter wants us to host them at the concert for a follow-up."

Sophia thought for a few seconds. "When I was in college, we read McLuhan, who wrote that the media is the message. Apparently social media is now the message. How is the event coming together?"

"I think it should be a good one. The talent has been lining up and the technical sound and lighting guys are working today. I'll start rehearsing my songs tomorrow."

"Everybody at school wishes you the best. In a little over a week, our classes for the year will be over."

"Uh-oh, Gerry's calling. I should take this. I'll call you, kisses."

Michael's phone clicked off before Sophia could reply. She sat down on a bench in front of the farmhouse, thinking to herself. "This is his world...I guess it will always come first." Sophia let out a big sigh, went inside and called out.

"Michele, want to go to Pizzeria Poppi Ivano with me?"

Michele came running out putting on his jacket. Sophia smiled and gave him a hug.

"I'll get the car keys."

On Monday morning, Michael was at the Teatro Sistina, which was a beautiful place to hold large events in Rome. He liked to be early during rehearsals to meet with his sound and lighting techs. As he went onto the stage, a voice from the audience interrupted his preparation.

"Michael Ventura...they told me you would be an early

bird."

Michael looked out to see who was calling him. He signaled for the lighting tech to switch the lights to the seats. A beautiful woman came quickly up the aisle.

"It's me, Vanessa...I hope I haven't changed so much you don't recognize me."

Michael quickly left the stage and went to meet her. "Vanessa! You haven't changed at all, still as gorgeous as ever. What brings you to Rome?"

"Long story, short version. My TV series got cancelled about seven years ago. Since then, I had a few cameos, one failed pilot. When I went to auditions, I was a pretty face when they wanted someone more average-looking. Of course, there were a few creeps who were interested because they wanted me in their bed. I became very discouraged and moved home. Been singing at some small clubs, mostly around the New York metro area. My father even got me a few gigs where you were discovered."

"Frankie's?"

"Yep. They were very nice to me, even complimentary, but it didn't change my situation. My dad had Mary pull a few strings for me to perform at this event. He said with you as the headliner, it would get lots of publicity."

"Nobody told me, but you are a most welcome addition to the program. You should check in with Giuseppe. He's a stickler about personally meeting all the performers."

"It's covered. I only flew in this morning from New York. I didn't even stop to change; thought I'd check out this place before meeting him for lunch. If this gig doesn't work for me, I don't know what I'll do."

"Look it's good you are here. This is a big deal from a publicity standpoint, with television, streaming services involved and social media ready to light up. Your dad is right, it should help get you noticed. Where are you staying?"

"That's another problem. He booked me at his friend's place in Monteverde because I'm on a tight budget, but beggars can't be choosers, right? How about you?"

"I'm booked at the Cavalieri, it's part of the Waldorf chain."

"Uhm...this is a little awkward, Michael. Would you mind if I clean up in your room, so I won't be late for my luncheon appointment? Mary told me in confidence that this Giuseppe guy wasn't so happy about my being here and I was also told he's big on being on time. I don't want to give him another reason to be unhappy by being late."

"I'll call the desk manager and tell him you're an important talent who just flew in and needs to change there. Please make a big deal giving him back the key card so we don't start any new rumors."

"Got it. Thank you so much for being so gracious, Michael. You've always been a good friend. Oh, I almost forgot to tell you how sorry I was to hear about your wife. I wanted to come but felt unworthy because of how I disappointed you. I hope you at least received my sympathy card."

"Your mom and dad came and told me why you weren't there. You did what you felt was right at the time. Please don't have regrets. I know what they can do to mess with your head—been there, done that myself."

Vanessa hugged him tightly and then broke away and walked quickly up the aisle. Michael watched her leave until she disappeared. What Michael didn't see was her tears. Before he went back on stage to rehearse, he stood for a minute, remembering that first special night with Vanessa. He was a little sad thinking that his old friend had been through some hard times. After rehearsing for several hours, Michael was exhausted and went back to his room at the hotel. After thinking over his decision, he called Gerry to tell him he wanted to help Vanessa by singing a duet with her.

"Michael that's not a good idea. Keep in mind that this is your come-back performance. It has to reflect your best. Remember, it will be televised and critiqued by all the media and music critics and most of all by your fans."

Michael held the phone for a minute thinking about Gerry's cautionary words. Though he knew they were based on logic and years of experience in a volatile business, he decided to do the duet with Vanessa. When he told her, she started crying, because having a duet with him would be an instant boost to her career. Michael even suggested a song that would show her vocal ability to demonstrate a song's emotional core. Vanessa readily agreed with his suggestion that they sing a powerful melancholy song, "Help me Make it Through the Night."

Michael scheduled the rehearsal and invited Gerry to be there. He asked Gerry to evaluate the emotional impact of singing it with Vanessa and if he thought their chemistry would appeal to the audience. When Michael introduced Vanessa onstage for the rehearsal, Gerry liked their look together. As they took their microphones, Vanessa thanked him with a nodding gesture. As soon as the orchestra hit the right note, he began singing the first two verses then nodded to Vanessa who sang, then they played off each other's lead with a slight nod.

When they finished, everyone in the theater was clapping. Gerry was standing and clapping enthusiastically, impressed by how well they performed together. There were tears in Vanessa's eyes as she grasped Michael's hand while they took a bow. All the rehearsals that week went very well,

Gerry was so pleased with how everything was going, he invited everyone involved to come to the hotel for a pre-concert party. He announced that the concert was already a sold-out success and donations for the charities were pouring in.

The celebration was at the hotel's smaller ballroom. The performers and their handlers were having a good time socializing and meeting the influential entertainment executives that Gerry invited. Michael was watching the festivities from a table, sipping a glass of wine and enjoying that everyone was feeling good. He was happy the rehearsals went so well, especially his duet with Vanessa. He was so impressed with her emotional interpretation; he began thinking of putting the duet with Vanessa on his next album. He was also gratified that Gerry was happy with their performance since he respected his cautionary advice. When Michael felt a tap on his shoulder, he turned to see Vanessa glowing and beautiful in her body-hugging gown. She was slightly inebriated but trying not to show it.

"You made it happen for me. I've already had some interest from nice people that Gerry sent over. I can't thank you enough, especially after the way I blew you off for Jeff. You haven't changed at all, have you? You're still the same nice guy you were in high school."

Michael stood up and steadied Vanessa by holding her by the shoulders. "I wasn't such a good person before I met you. It took my mother to remind me to do the right thing. You were a loving friend who taught me about performing and loving. You always encouraged me when I wasn't so sure. When we rehearsed the duet, you had such emotion singing that song with me that you had the audience in tears. To be honest, while we sang together, I had to control myself from tearing up myself."

Vanessa started sniffling. "Singing that song with you, Michael, made me miss what we had years ago. All I could think of was you and me and that first special night and all the others we shared. At the end of that song, I also had to control myself. Gerry told me that you overrode him to sing it with me."

"I told you a long time ago we would always be good friends."

Vanessa put her arms around Michael and pressed him against her. "My father thanks you, my mother thanks you, my sister thanks you, but most of all I thank you."

Michael smiled. "Wait a minute...you don't have a sister, and that's a line from an old musical?"

"Yep. Jimmy Cagney, *Yankee Doodle Dandy*. I think 1940-something. I wasn't a musical theater major in college for nothing and always loved that line."

"You're a crazy person but a very special one."

Vanessa gave him a long kiss on the lips surprising Michael who reacted instinctively by pulling his head back. "Sorry, Michael. I'm a little drunk and very grateful."

Vanessa broke away and quickly disappeared into the crowd of revelers. Still somewhat perplexed by Vanessa's emotional kiss, Michael suddenly thought of Sophia. He looked at his watch. It was almost midnight. He took out his cellphone and texted her to check if she was awake and would like to have a quick Zoom meeting. Sophia answered with an enthusiastic "Yes!"

Michael quietly slipped out of the party and went up to his room. As he started to open his door, Vanessa came rushing along to him from the other end of the corridor.

"I wanted to again apologize for embarrassing you at the party. I never could hold my liquor as they say. Now I can't go to stay at the Fienberg's. He and his wife are very religious and strictly forbid drinking. I hate to ask but could I crash on your couch."

"Vanessa, that's not a good idea, but come in and I'll help you."

As they entered, Michael saw that Vanessa was a little wobbly on her feet.

"Please sit, and I'll make a call."

"I have to use the bathroom...the booze."

"Back there by the bedroom."

When Vanessa was gone, Michael called the front desk.

"Hi, this is Michael Ventura...I'm calling because one of our performers needs a room for the night."

After a long pause, Michael pumped his fist.

"That would be great, put it on my bill. Her first name is Vanessa. I'll tell her to see you and bring her passport."

Michael opened his laptop to Zoom online with Sophia. When she signed in, she looked concerned.

"Michael, I thought you were going right to the room. What happened?"

"Long story, an old friend needed my help. I'll tell you about it later after I get her settled."

Just then Vanessa, who was still a little woozy, came out of the bathroom and over to Michael as he was talking to Sophia on his laptop.

"Sophia, I'd like you to meet Vanessa. She'll be performing at the concert. She and her dad are old friends from New York."

Vanessa's eyes widened looking at Sophia on the Zoom connection, as did Sophia looking back at the beautiful woman in Michael's room.

"Nice meeting you, Sophia. Michael has been a wonderful and kind friend. I don't think we met before...or did we?"

Sophia was still confused by Vanessa's presence. "I'm sure I would have remembered you. Michael didn't tell me about you till now, but good luck on your performance. It's for a great cause."

"Singing with Michael has been a blessing."

"I wasn't aware of that either. Lots of surprises. I'm sure you'll both do very well."

Michael interrupted. "Vanessa, you should go now and bring your passport to the main desk. They have a room and don't worry about the bill."

Vanessa understood and nodded, tapped Michael on the head as a friendly gesture, picked up her handbag and left the room. Sophia was still puzzled about what just happened.

"Michael, what was that all about?"

"Short version: Vanessa, as you might guess, is a little tipsy and staying at her dad's friend's house. The friend and his wife are negative about alcohol use, so I got her a room for the night."

"You do know how crazy this would sound to people. First you pay for a party of women you don't know at a restaurant, then you pay for a room for a beautiful female friend who comes out of your bedroom apparently a little drunk. Plus, she is someone you are going to sing a duet at this important concert."

"When you put it that way, I guess it does sound a little crazy. At the time I was doing what I did made sense to me. Incidentally, Vanessa came out of the bathroom not the bedroom. Sophia, I'm sorry I hadn't brought you up to date about the duet with Vanessa or helping her with a room for the night, but I can't live my life in fear of how others interpret what I do that might be considered a little nuts."

"By the way, speaking of being more than a little crazy, Tina also told me yesterday that you gave them a very generous check at the wedding."

"That was my pleasure, and it wasn't that big."

Sophia thought for a moment. "You know what's even crazier than all this? I think I finally understand you. You have these generous instincts like your grandfather and unlike most people, you aren't afraid to do them. So, if a room full of women want to hug you or a beautiful, inebriated woman comes out of your bathroom, it's just another day in the life of Michael Ventura."

Michael laughed and went up close to the laptop screen.

"Thank you for understanding me since I don't understand myself. Now I must go to sleep because there are only three more days before the concert. You get some rest and give my best to your students when you wrap up the year."

Sophia put her face close to her screen. "There is no way I'm going to tell the girls in my class you were thinking of them. They would drive me looney and I won't say break a leg to you. With my luck, it would happen and ruin the next time we get together. I'm sending you a more than friendly good luck kiss until we can do more than kiss digitally on our computers."

Sophia puckered her lips and blew a kiss then quickly signed off, leaving Michael with a contented smile.

Chapter 23

CHRISTMAS SURPRISE

On December 23, Sophia and her colleagues were in the teacher's room on the last day of classes saying their goodbyes before the Christmas break. Anna came over to Sophia who was pensive and looking a little sad as she collected her belongings to leave.

"Are you going down to Rome to see Michael's concert performance? Some teachers and staff bought a block of tickets because we thought we should go to support him as he helped us."

Sophia smiled but had a distant look in her eyes.

"I'm glad you all did. Michael and I Zoomed a few days ago. He called me yesterday and asked if I would come. I said I would see because of Michele. It's Christmas and he only has one parent right now. I'm still not sure if I should go. Michael will be surrounded by his fans and the media will be all over it. This is an important time for him to focus on his career. Remember, he stopped performing when his wife was sick. After she died, he didn't feel emotionally able to perform many of his popular songs. This Christmas Eve concert is a first step."

Anna gently gripped Sophia's shoulder. "I think what he needs is Sophia to be with him this Christmas. Isn't that the message in a popular American song?"

Sophia laughed. "I'm not sure the world-famous Michael Ventura needs his old friend Sophia more than his legions of adoring fans for Christmas. Come, let's enjoy our holiday break."

"I also wanted to thank you for pushing Matteo my way. He's been a real gentleman. He's kind, generous and affectionate, but I'm afraid he's still his Momma's boy. I'm not sure where our relationship will end up but meanwhile, I'm enjoying his company and going to great restaurants."

"Sounds like a mature way to deal with it."

Sophia took Anna's arm and walked her out of the building. Some teachers were already outside chatting and others were right behind. They were all enjoying the unusually warm day for late December when suddenly there was a loud sound in the distance.

Everyone stopped talking and looked toward the sky where a loudspeaker was blasting "Santa Claus is Coming to Town," as a helicopter came roaring into view. The teachers, staff and a few students in the parking area were riveted watching the low flying helicopter land in the school's parking lot. The passenger door opened as the blades stopped spinning. Michael jumped down, sporting a red Santa hat. Looking over to the school, he saw the crowd looking at him curiously.

Anna squealed with delight, took Sophia by the arm, and pulled her toward Michael, who was walking quickly toward them. Sophia, who was still in shock at his dramatic arrival, shouted,

"Michael! You need to be in Rome for your Christmas concert."

Michael jogged quickly over to Sophia. "Truthfully, if I can borrow from Mariah's wonderful song, all I need for Christmas is you. To make my wish come true, you and Michele are coming with me to Rome as soon as I bring you to yours and you two get packed."

Sophia was speechless. Michael pointed to his Santa hat.

"It's the hat. Too much, isn't it?"

Sophia laughed. "The hat's okay but you're more than a little pazzo. Are you sure you want Michele and me tagging along?"

Michael leaned in, touched her hair in a loving way then lovingly embraced and kissed her. "Of course I'm sure!"

Sophia put her arms tightly around his neck and kissed his face furiously. When they broke apart, Michael put his arms around her shoulder and ushered her quickly toward the helicopter.

"One more thing. Do you remember the last time we visited Mr. Schmidt's wonderful villa and property?"

"Of course. On the way back from Tina's wedding. That's a truly amazing place."

"Would you like to live there with Michele?"

"What are you saying?"

"We'll talk about it on the way."

Michael took Sophia by the hand, and he lifted her onto the waiting helicopter. He stopped to give a last wave to the onlookers who cheered.

Notes

The following songs were featured in "Siena My Love":

"The Way You Look Tonight." Jerome Kern with lyrics from Dorothy Fields-Singer, Frank Sinatra

"What A Wonderful World." Music, lyrics by George David Weiss and Bob Thiele-Singer, Louis Armstrong

"Got A Lot of Livin' To Do & Honestly Sincere." Ben Weisman, *Bye, Bye Birdie*. First Recorded by Elvis Presley.

"All I Do Is Dream of You." Otto Harbach, Oscar Hammerstein II, Frank Mandel Music: Sigmund Romberg -Singers Debbie Reynolds- Dean Martin- Michael Bublé

"That's Amore." Composer Harry Warren-Singer Dean Martin

"Catch a Falling Star." Composers, Paul Vance &Lee Pockriss-Singer, Perry Como

"Fly me to the Moon." Composer, Bart Howard-Singers, Kay Ballard, Frank Sinatra

"Smile." Composer Charlie Chaplin-Singer, Nat King Cole

"Help Me Make It Through the Night." Composer Kris Kristofferson-Singers, Willie Nelson, Elvis Presley

"Feeling Good." Composers Anthony Newley & Lesly Bricusse, Singer Anthony Newley, Nina Simone

"When I Fall in Love." Composer Victor Young, Lyrics Gordon Jenkin-Singers Nat King Cole, Michael Bublé

"Santa Clause is Coming to Town." Composers J. Fred Coots & Haven Gillespie-Singer, Bing Crosby, Michael Bublé

NOTE: Many of these great oldies have been performed by other very talented singers; a worthwhile treasure hunt.

About Atmosphere Press

Atmosphere Press is an independent, full-service publisher for excellent books in all genres and for all audiences. Learn more about what we do at atmospherepress.com.

We encourage you to check out some of Atmosphere's latest releases, which are available at Amazon.com and via order from your local bookstore:

Dancing with David, a novel by Siegfried Johnson

The Friendship Quilts, a novel by June Calender

My Significant Nobody, a novel by Stevie D. Parker

Nine Days, a novel by Judy Lannon

Shadows of Robyst, a novel by K. E. Maroudas

Home Within a Landscape, a novel by Alexey L. Kovalev

Motherhood, a novel by Siamak Vakili

Death, The Pharmacist, a novel by D. Ike Horst

Mystery of the Lost Years, a novel by Bobby J. Bixler

Bone Deep Bonds, a novel by B. G. Arnold

Terriers in the Jungle, a novel by Georja Umano

Into the Emerald Dream, a novel by Autumn Allen

His Name Was Ellis, a novel by Joseph Libonati

The Cup, a novel by D. P. Hardwick

The Empathy Academy, a novel by Dustin Grinnell

Tholocco's Wake, a novel by W. W. VanOverbeke

Dying to Live, a novel by Barbara Macpherson Reyelts

Looking for Lawson, a novel by Mark Kirby

Yosef's Path: Lessons from my Father, a novel by Jane Leclere Doyle

About the Author

Tom Bisogno grew up in Brooklyn, NY and loved listening to the celebrity singers of the old standards genre. He spent several summer vacations near Siena, Italy with his family, which inspired *Siena My Love.* His first novel was a self-published story titled *Leave Six Inches...* With his wife, Louisa Burns-Bisogno, he also co-authored a stage play, *Love Signs,* for a deaf theater group, and a prime-time television movie for CBS, *Bridge to Silence,* which starred Marlee Matlin. His screenplay *Sleuthhound* was presented at the HBO theater after it was selected by the National Academy of Television and Science. Currently, Tom is writing a screenplay and has completed several chapters of a non-fiction book.

Tom has a BA in English and an MBA in Marketing and had a varied career in accounting and marketing management with a major corporation, as a partner in a real estate company and as a communication and life skills instructor at WCSU and at Iona, Marist, and Dominican colleges.